LEDFEATHER

LEDFEATHER
STEPHEN GRAHAM JONES

FC2

TUSCALOOSA

The University of Alabama Press
Tuscaloosa, Alabama 35487-0380

Published by FC2, an imprint of the University of Alabama Press, with support provided by Florida State University, the Publications Unit of the Department of English at Illinois State University, and the School of Arts and Sciences, University of Houston–Victoria

Address all editorial inquiries to: Fiction Collective Two, University of Houston–Victoria, School of Arts and Sciences, Victoria, TX 77901-5731

⊗

The paper on which this book is printed meets the minimum requirements of American National Standard for Information Sciences—Permanence of Paper for Printed Library Materials, ANSI Z39.48–1984

Library of Congress Cataloging-in-Publication Data
Jones, Stephen Graham, 1972-
   Ledfeather / by Stephen Graham Jones. — 1st ed.
     p. cm.
   ISBN-13: 978-1-57366-146-1 (pbk. : alk. paper)
   ISBN-10: 1-57366-146-5 (pbk. : alk. paper)
   1. Indian boys—Fiction. 2. Blackfeet Indian Reservation (Mont.)—Fiction. I. Title.
   PS3560.O5395L43 2008
   813'.54—dc22
                                        2007049044

Book Design: Andrew Farnsworth and Tara Reeser
Cover Design: Lou Robinson
Typeface: Baskerville
Produced and printed in the United States of America

for Rane—

    Aoh ma ta kit   noh ko wa

and for Dodd, who did

Between 1856 and 1907, when the tribal rolls were settled, the Blackfeet endured some twenty-four federally appointed Indian Agents. Of them, Francis Dalimpere had the shortest term: fourteen months. He arrived in September of 1883. It was his first "Western" posting. He was thirty-two.

I remember you.

We thought he was dead already just when he opened the door. Junior looked at me from behind the counter and I knew what he was asking: if I'd put the sign up or not? We were supposed to be closed was the thing. He'd already turned the grill off and loaded everything back in the freezer and locked it. All I was doing was lining up bottled waters in the short cooler. It was what we were having to make tea from that week, because it was the second snow already, before the first even usually came, and in East Glacier, you get that kind of wet in the ground and everybody's driving into Browning to take their showers, because the water from the tap runs brown.

Instead of pulling the door shut, too, that kid, that Doby Saxon whose mom had married that crazy Yellowtail who didn't even have an Indian name anymore, he just stood there like he was waiting for permission to come in, waiting for me or Junior to say to him it was okay if he had the snow crusted all over him still, that he could stomp it off in here if he wanted, that we'd mop it up later.

But then I looked to what he was looking at.

It was the back door, all the way through the dining room.

Because the front door was open, the back door was rattling, like somebody was trying to get in, or had just left. I'm not even sure the kid knew we could see him.

I started to say something but Junior held his hand up to me flat and sudden, his palm to the ground, a cut off motion I'd only ever seen him use once before, in a bar over in Havre, right before one cowboy stabbed another cowboy in the neck with some shiny kind of cow tool I'd never seen.

I sucked my cheeks in, went stiff, ready to walk away like we'd had to then—because stabbed-in-the-neck cowboys aren't something an Indian can run away from in Montana—and didn't even look up to Junior when he said whatever he said to the kid. It was Indian, two words maybe, or one long one, and I was pretty sure Junior only knew four or five all told, most of them having to do with cigarettes, because sometimes that's the only way to get an old man to give you one, is to ask right.

What he said now, though, I don't think it had anything to do with cigarettes. I asked him later what it translated out to and he said he didn't remember saying it, but he was lying. I mean, I could go down to the old people's home in Browning right now and, if I said whatever he said that night to Doby Saxon, I think every wrinkled old face in that room, that hasn't even recognized their own kids for twenty years, every one of them would turn to me, to see if this white woman was really saying that, and where did she hear it?

And did the kid understand what Junior said?

I don't know.

With Malory Sainte for a mom and a Yellowtail dad, he probably just knows cartoons and whatever you can learn from the label of a beer bottle. The only Indian they would have talked around him would have been about car starters and pawn stubs.

The kid did at least turn to the sound of Junior's voice, and that's when I saw that his truck wasn't parked out on the curb, or across the street. The street was empty.

My face went hot and for the thousandth time I was glad I'd never had any kids on the reservation, because this is what happens. They drive off every road they can, and then, because it hasn't started hurting yet, whichever one can still walk does, to the nearest light, his face packed with windshield glass.

But then I was running to him like he was my own son anyway, like they all were, and I was pulling him through the door, trying to get all the snow off at once, see where he was broken.

When I looked up to Junior, instead of calling the ambulance he was looking where the kid had been looking, at the back door, like some other Indian had just walked through, out, and he was trying to remember who it had been but it had been too long already.

He came back to me just as lost as the kid, then nodded slow like he does, pulled the phone off its rack.

This is how a night can start to last forever up here.

Inside of two minutes we had the table pulled out from one of the booths and the two bench seats pushed together, and the kid's chin wasn't even shaking, and that's not good.

"Where are they?" I said to him, close to his face, trying to give him all the warmth I'd ever had, all the bodyheat he needed, and he focused his eyes down on me like he was try-ing to make sense of my words, or just be sure I was real, but then he went blank again, just staring through me, and over the next hour and a half his clothes finally started to melt, and a pool formed around him, for us to mop up later.

It wasn't just snow, though.

The seats are orange so it was hard to tell at first, and the floor's just that varnished wood you can't tell anything with, but when Junior dipped his other dish towel down into the meltoff, it came back red, bloody, like that one side of the kid's face.

"Hold on," I said to him, "we called, they're coming. You made it."

This was the Blackfeet Reservation on a Saturday night in late November, though.

By the time the ambulance got there, it was Thanksgiving.

I didn't go to the hospital for Doby Saxon, I went to the hospital for his dad. But then every cop on the reservation was in the hall there, and one of them was asking me if I could do a test for them maybe?

I told him it was my day off, thanks.

He asked back what I was doing up there then?

I shrugged, lifted my chin hey to a nurse I knew.

The truth is that I was already doing a test, on my own time. I wanted to see if Earl Two Jobs—he'd made the name up himself—was a real Yellowtail like everybody said, if he was going to try to sneak into the hospital to see his only son, who was probably dying from exposure. I didn't ask, but I was pretty sure Earl had a couple of bench warrants out on him. But game wardens don't serve bench warrants.

Why I wanted to see him had to do with two elk racks that had shown up down in Great Falls over the summer. The warden down there had sent me the pictures because he knew that tines don't get thick like that just on state grass. What it takes for postcard racks like he'd seized was some kind of preserve, the National Park kind. Glacier. And this time, finally, the horns had been sawed right out of the skull, so nobody was going to be saying they were sheds, and the way I knew they weren't taken out in Landslide or some other part of Region 1, which is year-round, is that I have the two cut-open skulls in the vented box behind the office. More than that, I knew those two old bulls, had been glassing them since May.

When the fires hit Tar Ridge in late July, up past Volly's, almost all the way to that second lake up there, the bulls had walked down the Line and crossed the road into Boulder, and Boulder's off-limits all the time, unless you have twelve thousand dollars and a tribal guide. Unless you're white, basically.

I know the elk crossed into Boulder because that's where I found them, right there in Swiftcurrent Creek.

Somebody'd shot them from the road then hooked chains to them, dragged them halfway up onto the bank and gone to work on them with a chainsaw, just taking the hindquarters and the horns and the eyeteeth, probably driving away without any headlights even, because all the old poachers up here, they don't need lights to know where the roads are.

As to why I wanted to talk to Earl Two Jobs about this—his born name's Piney Saxon, and I don't know what joker made that up—it's that he was on that hotshot crew that went up to Volly's in July, to stomp out the fire, keep it from crossing the Line into Glacier, where it would become a natural burn. And I can just see him riding in the back of that truck for two, three days in a row, watching those monster elk just standing there in the shallows, their racks mossy with velvet.

Him and the rest of the crew would have been sighting down through the scopes of their imaginary rifles and making jokes, sure, but only one of them had come back that night.

The reason I liked Earl Two Jobs for it is that when he came in for his tags in September he had a new rifle hooked over his shoulder, too expensive to leave in the truck for even five minutes.

Racks like the ones from Great Falls would pull anywhere from five to fifteen hundred dollars.

"Each one of these good for what, six head?" I'd asked him, passing the sheet of tags over.

He'd laughed, his blunt tongue pushed between his teeth.

If he was just getting meat, I could understand. This is land we've been hunting since before America was America, I mean, and if we don't manage the Glacier herd, the cows will all be starving come January.

But when it starts to be about money, when you're just grabbing some meat because the saw's out anyway, then, yeah, I come up to the hospital on Thanksgiving, maybe wait for you.

The hours went by though, no Earl Two Jobs, and all there was to do was watch football in the waiting room and wait to see if Doby was going to live or become a statistic. They still hadn't found his car, didn't even know who'd been with him. Some snowplow driver would see something in a week or two, we all figured. If not, then the car would show up when the snow melted off, and we could have another funeral.

"Well then," I finally said to everybody at halftime, and ducked out, nearly walked right into Malory Sainte.

She drew her lips in tight—her sister does that too, and I think it has something to do with getting locked up so much—had been crying it looked like, and just stared at me the way Indian moms can do when somebody has to take the blame.

I knew better than to say anything, just stepped aside, let her pass.

But then I couldn't leave either.

Parked out in handicapped, the door still open like she'd just left it, was Earl's truck. His little flatbed trailer was dragging behind it, empty.

Because Malory didn't know how to unhitch it, or because she didn't want to unhitch it?

The second, I thought. She was dragging the trailer around because she was going to need it.

I swept the snow from the driver's seat for her and shut the door, looked to the hospital to see if she was watching. She wasn't. I nodded, followed my hand down the bed rail.

The trailer was shopmade, just wide enough for two snowmobiles.

I looked north, to the clouds stacking up around Chief Mountain, then kicked the ice sludge from behind her rear tire and went back inside.

"Test?" I said to the cop who'd asked.

"Thought you were off today?" he said back.

"Hunting season," I told him. "Twenty-four seven."

He finished his plate of turkey and got me to follow him down to a black trash bag. It was all the clothes they'd cut from Doby Saxon.

The cop untied the bag then stood, let me see.

The clothes were soggy with blood.

"His?" I said, because I couldn't smell it yet.

"Not a cut on him," the cop said back.

"And you want to know…?"

"Do you have some test to tell if it's human or not?"

Which is how I ended up with the bag in the bed of my truck.

Just down from the hospital and the clinic, on Death Row where all the elders and their families lived, I stopped in the middle of the road, untied the bag, let the smell I'd already caught mix with the woodsmoke in the air.

Not ten minutes later, every dog in Browning was pawing my truck. Because they'd been trained on this, knew the smell, knew that, when a truck pulls in with this kind of scent coming from the back, there's going to be shortshanks and heads and maybe even the skin.

The blood Doby Saxon had been soaked in wasn't human, but game.

Earl Two Jobs had gotten Malory to drop him and Doby off on some logging road over near the Line, Livermore probably, where the marker's always bent down, and then they'd eased their snowmobiles into Glacier to hunt the Mineral Strip like the elders still say you're supposed to be able to. And maybe they're right. But, if we look the other way for that, then people are going to be popping mule deer out in the Sweetgrass Hills too, and after that, all of Montana probably, and it'll be war again, and there's not enough of us yet for that.

I don't know.

I was sure of one thing that day anyway: I wouldn't get to pin a ticket to Earl Two Jobs that season. Or ever.

He should have checked the weather before he slipped across the Line.

The maps had been frozen white for days.

I would have stayed if he would have asked me to. If we were just there at the casino to collect his mom again. Even to just walk through, because we *could*. I'd hit eighteen four months ago. But Doby said this was him, that he had to do this.

Out at the edge of the parking lot he spread all his ID cards out on the dash of my car, then picked out his own.

The rest were for the liquor store, for videos, for off-rez, for wherever one Indian was the same as all the rest.

The casino's different, though.

If their shiny new gambling license gets pulled, then fifty or a hundred people lose their jobs like that, come looking for whoever let that minor in the door. And then they go looking for that minor too.

So, yeah, we'd been in before, but with escorts, and just to peel Malory Sainte up from some table. Once Doby had to talk her out of the security room even, with the real cops on the way and everything.

I don't remember what the charges against her were going to be that time. Probably destruction of property, maybe a PI. Both, more. That whole family, man, they're Yellowtail through and through. Give them three dollars and instead of a loaf of bread, they'll rub those three bills fast between their hands and then lay them down on some nappy green table, because this time it's going to work.

And when it doesn't, it's everybody else's fault.

That time his mother was in the box, though, Doby sucked his cheeks in like he can when he's trying to look especially Indian—the main security guy was white—and told him the story of how the woman locked behind that door had sat by his bed in the hospital for nine weeks once, holding his hand, making him live. That she'd sung to him songs buried so deep that it tore her up inside, permanently, songs she didn't even know she had, that her grandmother probably hadn't even known, songs that kept him alive when the doctors had given up, when he had *wanted* to give up.

But Malory Sainte never did.

She'd lost her husband that winter. She wasn't about to lose her son.

So, handing her over to the cops like the security guy wanted to do, what it would mean is her getting locked up for a month or two away from him. It would be the same as if he'd just died on the mountain four years ago. Her son would be gone from her anyway, the one she'd fought for, the one that shouldn't even be alive anymore.

As far as I know, too, talking to that white security guard, that's the first time Doby ever said it out loud like that, that he shouldn't be alive, that he should have died up in Glacier with his dad.

It's a bad thing to start thinking.

Before, all I'd ever heard of it—not that hunting trip, he never talked about that to anybody, not even his mom, and the snowmobiles never showed up, Earl either—all I'd ever heard was this bullshit paper our English teacher from Arizona had made us write.

Doby took hackysack for his subject, a joke, and then wrote about standing in a circle with me and Tone and Jamie at Indian Days, keeping the bag alive. How when he was playing it, and had the right cigarette in his mouth, he could focus only on that ounce or two of sand and leather, and how sometimes he would look up while the bag was in the air and see that he was all alone for miles, that Browning wasn't even around him anymore, and how that was all right too.

And I only ever heard about that because our Arizona English teacher read it to the class when Doby wouldn't.

Halfway through, he walked out.

I followed him that day, and kept following, through all the shit, the rolled-over cars and beer bottles to the back of the head and fires we didn't know anything about and the walking back to town at four in the morning, the northern lights so hard and pink we even had watery shadows on the asphalt once. It made us feel like ghosts after about a quarter mile of it, and we started walking over in the grass instead.

They were the same though, our shadows. And I remember thinking that they maybe weren't going to be. Because, the way the old people looked at Doby, it was like he was different, like he was a deer who'd just walked into the IGA, and didn't really know he was a deer yet, that none of this was for him.

Crazier shit's happened.

As for what Doby had to do by himself at the casino, he'd showed me: two twenty-dollar bills he'd found rubberbanded in some medicine bottle at his house. He'd been looking for pills. The name on the bottle was his dad's, from when he'd been working some road crew and burned his hand or something. Pain meds. But then, instead, like his dad was giving them to Doby, telling him that it was special Indian money that couldn't lose, there were those two bills. Earl had just been waiting for Doby to turn eighteen, so we could cash in.

"But there wasn't even the casino four years ago," I'd said.

"That's what I'm saying, man," Doby'd cut back.

I'd just watched him.

I never knew Earl, but my mom says Doby looks just like him before he started drinking and his face got all pockmarked and beat-in.

At the drop-off for the casino—it's just like an emergency lane at the hospital—I told Doby that he owed Dally sixty for last weekend, yeah?

"Exactly," Doby said, and flashed the two twenties and his sharp-edged smile, like he was going to turn that forty into sixty easy, and then a hundred and a thousand and a new car that we'd never wreck up and have to fix behind my uncle's shop.

For a second, too, I think I believed him.

I guess it's why I followed him out of English that day.

He'd already lived through a night of seventy-below Montana winter, I mean. What could a pussy-ass English teacher from Arizona do to him? What could anybody?

"No Malories, man," I told him as he was climbing out.

He nodded, his bottom lip dragged up under his teeth into a different kind of smile, the kind that makes it impossible for a Yellowtail to hear anybody but himself, and then he was digging into his wallet for the ID card he'd just stashed, his keys coming up extra, spinning down to the ground, his right shoe slashing out like it had its own brain, stalling the keys on his toe.

Somewhere above them, Doby smiled a little bit more then bit it off, walked backwards into the casino, the guns his fingers had become held at his waist, so he could shoot me over and over, send me off right.

I shot him back once, over the wheel, and pulled away, my cheeks sucked in now too.

Those twenties were as good as gone.

He was just standing there on the other side of our RV. It was, I don't know, ten o'clock? Grant was talking to our waiter at the casino restaurant about how to get back up to the KOA. We'd done it in the daylight, of course, Duck Lake Road or something, but at night on that reservation you can't even see the mountains anymore. There aren't any houses up there, just trees and darkness. It feels like you're being watched.

Grant says I'm being silly, of course, that this is no different from anyplace else we've been, and he's probably right. Just earlier, in the gift shop thingy, Grant had been showing me how all these genuine Blackfeet artifacts had CHINA stamps on them. The girl behind the counter had been watching us though, listening, so I'd pretended not to have heard Grant, because that would be an insult to her people, wouldn't it? To laugh?

What I finally bought was a little stone tipi with Southwest designs on it and then a pack of postcards made from old brown and white pictures. Each one had a little history entry on back. It was the least I could do. The girl smiled when she gave me my change, and her teeth weren't perfect, no, but they were achingly beautiful, gave her just such personality. I hope she never fixes them.

After that I folded the top of my bag and walked down the aisles of slot machines, waiting for Grant to finish in the bathroom, but then saw that he was already having a conversation with the boy who'd been our waiter. They were pointing up and down imaginary roads, a five-dollar bill folded in Grant's hand as thanks, so I caught his eye, tilted my head outside to let him know I'd be at the RV. He nodded, never broke stride with the waiter.

When you've been married thirty-eight years, a look can be enough.

It's not what I dreamed about as a little girl, but it is what I dreamed about in my thirties. How we would get over these rough times, arrive finally at a place like this, and just know we were there for each other, that we had been all along.

The gentleman at the door opened it for me, thankfully, as I already had both hands full with the postcards.

I wasn't going to send any of them, I'd decided. Instead I was going to leave them on the coffee table so Charlene's kids could find them, carry them to me, ask if I really went there, their little voices so pure and so hopeful. What I'd do then—or I might have Grant trained for this part, as he needs roles sometimes, just to participate—would be to let the children look at each photograph while I read them the historical entry from the back. That way the Indian on the front could look back at them, and they could know his story a little bit. The good one, I mean.

That was part of why we were leaving already, even though Grant was still behind at his blackjack. There'd been a scene.

But I wasn't thinking about any of that ugliness. And it's not specific to Indians or reservations anyway. Sad things happen everywhere. The choice you have to make going through life is if you want to focus on them or not, whether you want to let them pull you down or whether you want to keep your chin up, a pleasant look on your face as you walk through the room.

It wasn't Grant's first instinct, to leave his chips all over the floor afterwards, walk away, but I think when he saw how I was having to hold my lips together, he understood, led me into the safety of the gift shop.

Like I said, we've been together thirty-eight years now.

So I nodded to the gentleman at the door and stepped through, flipping to the next postcard then reading its history as well, and was already through half the pack by the time I got to our RV and saw him there, not yet taking his next step, his eyes praying I belonged to some other car or truck.

It wasn't the first time I or Grant had walked onto somebody using the camper as a windbreak or a smoking area or just as a quiet place to talk on their phone, but it was the first time that the door was still swinging because it would no longer shut.

I breathed in sharp, my fist going to my throat like my mother's always did at bad news, and her mother's before her—heaven knows they each had enough of it—and the postcards fluttered down to the ground between us, and I laughed a little, I think.

The boy was the same one from the blackjack table. Grant had been sitting close to him for luck, because at first the boy had close to seven hundred dollars in chips and wasn't slowing down. Three times in a row, he hit twenty-one perfect, once even with five cards, until Grant told him not to use it all up there, yeah, kimosabe?

That's what Grant had been calling our waiter, kimosabe. It had been the joke all through dinner, until I'd had to cover my mouth with my napkin to laugh.

"Why not?" the boy said, still smiling, but not in a way I liked anymore.

Grant shrugged, his chips in his hands. "You only get so much, I mean," he said.

"So much what?"

"Luck."

The boy at the table thought it through and finally smiled, didn't sass Grant at all, like he probably deserved, but tapped two of his fifty-dollar chips on the table then traded them for another card, a king as it turned out. Grant shrugged like these things happen, because they do. But to the boy, that hand was an insult. And the next hand too, and the next, which he tried to make work by putting down more chips.

He was down to five chips—a hundred dollars—when this beautiful Indian woman suddenly appeared behind him.

All the other Indians in the area went quiet, even the dealer.

The boy knew without having to look around. He just tapped two of his chips out onto the felt and stared at his cards, then at the prescription bottle the woman set down on the table. And then he looked away from it.

What she asked him was if this was what he wanted, is this what he really wanted, is this what he walked through all that goddamn snow for?

The boy just chewed the inside of his cheek, didn't say anything.

When she said it all again, her voice cracking between the words, what the boy said back was that he'd learned from the best, yeah.

Now all the Indians in the area were looking at their hands.

The Indian woman nodded, her lip trembling, her eyes hard, and started humming something Indian to the boy. It made him look away, over the dealer's head, and then, like he was trying to stop her, he set his last two chips down on the table, nodded to the dealer, and took the jack that came next, and then that nine of diamonds that pushed him over, and when the dealer held his hand flat over the table, no more, the boy kept insisting, finally started pulling everything out from his pockets and fumbling it up onto the table for more cards, for that perfect card, that card that was going to let him win.

What he got instead was the pit boss's hand on his shoulder, pulling him away.

He spun out of it, stared up at the pit boss.

"Don't," the woman said to him then, to the boy, and the boy looked from her to the pit boss and all around, and was going to anyway. I have two sons myself, I mean. But I never could have done what that woman did next.

This doesn't mean I don't love them either, my boys.

I do.

But I'm not Indian, I guess. Maybe it's different with them? Something cultural?

"Hey, no—" Grant said, reaching for the boy, to stop this from happening, but I had his sleeve by then, and it was too late anyway. The boy was already swinging for the pit boss, the pit boss smiling that this was exactly what he'd been waiting for.

After the boy hit him, the pit boss threw him up onto the table, scattering Grant's chips everywhere. The boy slid into the dealer.

To get at him then, the pit boss had to step around the table.

He never made it, though.

Halfway there, his hand planted on one of the squares where the cards are supposed to go, the woman climbed onto his back, started hitting him in the neck with the side of her fist. The pit boss stumbled at first but then got his arm under him, threw the woman off.

She crashed into the stools behind us, wiped the blood from her teeth, and smiled the exact same smile the boy had been smiling earlier. That was when I clamped my hand onto Grant's arm, just to keep standing.

"You don't touch him," she said to the pit boss, slinging the blood away like it was nothing she wasn't used to. Like she was welcoming it, almost.

The boy was standing now. Breathing hard.

"Mom—" he said, but she shook her head no to him, fast, just once. All she said back was *Run, now.*

The boy just stared at her about this, so she said it again, for him to run, and then stood, pointing at the door, shaking her head no to him, that what he had to do was just run, and keep running, and never stop, and then the pit boss was to her and she was backing away, had a stool between them, was pushing its feet into the face of one slot machine, then another, throwing every bottle and glass she could find. One of them was plastic, still full of nickels. They clattered everywhere.

"Well?" she said to the pit boss.

"So this is how it is then," the pit boss said back, and she smiled, told him that this is the way it's always been, and only started running when she was sure he was coming for her.

Like I said, it's not something I could have done.

When I thought to look back to the blackjack table, the boy was gone. Until the parking lot anyway, all those postcards blowing between us. The door of our camper wrenched open behind him, something in his hand.

He held it out to me, and because—I think because that had been his mother inside, and I'd known it even before he said it—I took it.

It was just a bundle of crunchy animal skin tied together with rawhide. The whole thing was black with age. It hadn't been made in China.

Clipped to one of the rawhide strings was half an index card. I caught it, angled it over to catch the light from the casino:

```
moosehide(?)ceremon. bundle, ca.
1884, reclaimed from pwnshp(Kal)
1982. Contents attributed to
Dallimper, Fr(src: 'Sorrel' Lf Sr.)
see dis82b/Old Agency("Caligraph 2")
```

The stamp at the bottom of the tag read MUESUM OF THE PLAINS INDIAN. Then I remembered: the museum next door. I looked down along the side of the camper to it. We'd tried to go earlier like it said to in our packet but it had been shut down, the door dusty.

What the boy said to me then was *forty dollars*.

The hand he'd been holding the bundle with was bleeding, from whatever glass he'd punched through to steal the artifact.

"I—I—" I said, lowering myself all at once to the postcards.

He helped, collecting them with his good hand.

When we stood again, the bundle was on the ground between us.

He understood, nodded to himself about this and handed me the cards back, just stopping at the last instant to look at the top one, laugh a little.

"Tell your husband he was right," he said then, picking up the bundle, spiraling it up like a football, little pieces of leather crumbling off.

"If you—if you want I can…" I started, digging in my purse for the money anyway, for all of my money, but the boy was already shaking his head no, backing away, into the night.

I looked to where he'd been for a long time, and then to our busted door, and then to Grant, crossing the parking lot to me, his eyes on alert, because I shouldn't just be standing there.

Driving away twenty minutes later, the side door tied shut, we had to brake for the police sirens converging on the museum.

"Like they've got enough cops to fix this place," Grant said, and I looked down into my lap, to my postcards.

On top was one of the old time Indians, his skin brown and greasy, the fingers of his right hand wrapped around some spear or staff. What he was doing was staring hard into the camera like he knew what I'd done, what I hadn't done. The sign at his feet said GLACIER PARK INDIAN. Scratched into the print beside it like they used to do, his name, Yellow Tail.

I had to turn that postcard over.

Three hours later we were almost in North Dakota.

That waiter hadn't been our kimosabe after all.

Browning was a graveyard that night. That's the only reason we heard him. My sister muted the TV and looked outside. Not the front, where somebody would be about to knock on the window on their way to the door, but the back, where the basketball goal was.

He was out there shooting baskets.

We watched him through the back window for a few minutes, just two shadows behind a green curtain, backlit by the show.

"That's Doby Saxon," my sister finally said.

I was in sixth grade, but I knew who he was, sure.

The tips of three of his fingers on his right hand had been frozen off. One night behind the video store he'd caught me looking at them, his half-fingernails he probably didn't even have to cut anymore, and then he'd held them up so I could see better.

"Why just them?" I'd asked him.

I was in fifth grade then, was still stupid.

Doby had shrugged, taken another pull off his beer—he was sitting on a board across the top of the trashcan—and looked down to his dumb cousin Robbie. He was trying to teach some of the other fifth graders stick game, but making them use real dimes and quarters.

"Because I had to hold it shut at first," Doby said, looking at his hand too, and then held his beer out to me.

I shook my head no, my eyes all narrow because I was cool. I couldn't figure out what to do with my mouth, though.

After a while of watching Doby Saxon shoot baskets and chase the ball through the grass and spare parts, my sister went back to the couch.

I'd seen that show though.

What I was doing was trying to figure out if Doby Saxon had to hold the ball any different, missing three fingertips like that.

Finally he made two in a row from the same place and smiled to himself, fancy dribbled back to the back of the concrete, turned and shot.

He was pretending he was playing somebody.

And he was crying too.

I could see it sometimes when he'd try to do a spin move, lose the ball out into the grass again.

Who was he playing?

It's stupid to ask, I know—like he's going to answer, now—but it's the only thing to ask, too.

If I were playing out there at night by myself and pretending somebody was guarding me, it would probably be my brother Jet, from before he got locked up in Seattle. And, instead of being mad when I shot one over him, made it, he'd be happy, slap the ball between his hands, tell me to do that again, yeah?

Nobody knows I saw him that night anyway, Doby Saxon, even though the next day at school everybody was talking about him.

It's not like it's a secret or anything, it's just that, and this is stupid, I know, but I make deals.

My deal that night, watching Doby Saxon shoot baskets in our backyard, was that if he made four in a row this time, then Jet would get early parole, and if he only made three, then we'd get to drive out and see him, and if it was only two then Jet would write back. But if it was just one—

It's not my fault, what Doby Saxon did after he left our house.

At least I don't think so.

If it was only one shot in a row though, which is no row at all, then it was supposed to be on him, on Doby Saxon. That's the way I called it in my head.

And I gave him as many chances as possible, changing the rules each time he missed, but it was like he was doing it to himself on purpose almost.

"What already?" my sister said to me.

I shook my head no, nothing, then went to the kitchen without turning the light on, creaked the back door open.

Doby Saxon dribbled once and caught the ball, looked across it to me, so that I could see somebody'd beat his face already that night.

"Little Step," he finally said.

It was what everybody called me instead of my real name.

I held out my dad's six-pack to him, to Doby Saxon. It was an apology, but he didn't know that, just looked at me, then dribbled one more time.

"You'll get in trouble," he finally said, and did a fallaway that banked in like money, like he was who everybody'd gone off to see that night.

"He won't remember," I told him back.

Doby Saxon caught the ball again, let it roll off into the grass for a horse to step on or something, then picked his way over to me, took the cardboard handle.

His eyes were still all messed up from crying, too. I don't think he knew I could tell. And there was blood all around his mouth. It was from his hand, I think.

Instead of letting go of my part of the handle, I called into the house for my sister, my voice shaking, and Doby Saxon tensed up.

She came out in her sweats with her headband on and just stared down at him.

"Amy," he said.

"Doby," she said back. "You're hurt."

He looked down to his hand, smiled like he was, yeah, then drank one of the beers while my sister wrapped his hand in a whole roll of gauze.

When she was done she took the beer from him, drank a long drink then gave it back.

He stood, looked north kind of.

Chief Mountain was up there somewhere, I guess. I'd been there once with Jet, to tie a shirt to a tree and not say anything. It was before he started going to Seattle. Everything was before he started going to Seattle.

"Holding what together?" I said to him then, to Doby Saxon.

He was at the edge of the house by then, about to turn back to the road, but stopped, held me in his eyes. Finally he remembered, held his blunt fingertips up.

"Holding what together?" I said again.

He laughed to himself a bit, shrugged, and said "Everything, I guess," then lifted his beer in thanks, walked away.

"Everything," I repeated to myself a few seconds later, and when I turned around to go back inside, one of the beers was still on the porch. He'd left it for me.

What I told myself was that if I could drink it all, then it would count for Jet somehow.

Halfway through, my sister was watching me through the screen door. Not even saying anything.

It's still the only beer I've ever drank.

We only came back because we'd never seen anybody die. Not in real life. And this, when Doby Saxon finally did it, it was going to be real life. Times two.

Unless he was just joking or something.

But as close as my uncle had come to hitting him—if it was a joke, then not many people were going to get it.

What he was doing was standing out at the first of Starr School, where everybody was still going fast, coming home all the way from Butte.

He was trying to step in front of those cars.

At first my Aunt Gracie had pointed to him like he was trying to flag us down, I think. There was this white stuff coming out from his hand like a flag, I mean. But then he just walked right out in front of us, his eyes open the whole time, his teeth pulled back from his lips for the impact, me and Chris screaming from the back seat.

The only reason my uncle didn't hit him was because he'd been drinking all night, so already had his hands ready for anything, even stupid Indians trying to kill themselves.

Not that he's not cute, Doby Saxon.

He's got enough Sainte blood in him that if he wasn't always with Robbie and the rest of those organ donors, I might even go out with him if he asked right.

But he's Yellowtail, too, so he'll never ask right, never go back to school, never hold down anything longer than a fence job or putting out fires.

Maybe that's why he was out there doing it, even.

Either that or his car was too busted up to drive it off Looking Glass like everybody else was doing that summer.

Two summers back, when Chris and me were freshman and Looking Glass was still closed, the train tracks had been the cool place to do it, or to let it happen anyway, and before that it had just been guns, mostly deer rifles that ended up getting buried too, scopes and slings and all, so that some of the graves got dug up when the first snows started coming.

And there was always just the slow way too, which I'd always figured Doby for, pretty much: old and looking like he'd lived through smallpox or something, his back to one of the empty storefronts, a bag in his hand with a bottle in it. The story of how he'd slipped into Glacier one night with his dad, and they'd shot every last elk in the Park but then got chased off each one, so that all they snuck back out with was the story.

Right beside him, too, there'd be the wino ghost of his dad, like they were sitting council, like no, Doby wasn't lying about those elk. It had really happened, only each of the elk had had racks that would hold a small car, horns that would rip holes in the sky if that elk turned his head wrong.

The story he wouldn't tell, probably, would be the one about the time his friend Jamie OD'd in that concrete tipi down by Aunt Gracie's old house, and him and Robbie tried to bring him back by giving him some more.

That year at Indian Days, I remember the whole high school had to follow Jamie's framed picture two times around the dance circle while the drums counted out our steps.

It was supposed to teach us something, make us really understand.

Afterwards, though, there were Robbie and Doby out behind the booths, drinking beer from plastic cups and playing stupid hackysack like nothing had even happened.

We just watched them for a while, until Doby saw us, started watching us back.

Finally he caught their hackysack in his hand, crumpled his empty cup up and walked away, into all the feathers and bustles and cotton candy.

I don't know.

We were going to be the ones to see it, anyway. Because we'd already tried talking to him, after my uncle circled back around, the air still just floating with dirt and grass.

He was drunk though, Doby, was like a deer or something. Every time we started to open the doors, he'd float towards the fence, to run away with whatever that thing was he was carrying. It looked like a stepped-on football, or a shriveled-up dog head.

The last thing Gracie said to him through the window was that she was calling Malory on him. That Malory was going to come out here.

Doby had called back his home phone number to us, then laughed about it.

"They should put a sign up," my uncle said, driving

away, watching Doby in the rear view, "Drunk Indian Crossing." Gracie put her hand on his forearm then. It was her way of telling him he was right, but he shouldn't be saying that kind of stuff either. "But then they'd need one every few feet!" he added, laughing at himself, and Gracie shook her head, took her hand back.

"They're already there," she said, low so we could hardly hear.

What she was talking about was her first group of kids, from Thomas, her first husband.

Two of their markers were in the ditches on the reservation, with feathers hanging off them to show they were still Indian anyway, that nobody was taking that away.

We didn't say anything from the backseat, just filed into the house, out Chris's window in our coats, then walked through Starr School out to the pasture by the road.

A car was coming.

Chris was holding my hand now.

We hadn't ever seen anybody die was the thing. And it wasn't so funny now.

"Go," I said to her, nodding ahead of us, and Chris looked over to me, ahead to the car—she had medals for the eight-hundred and the mile, all the way back from junior high—and then she was gone like smoke, my hand even still holding the shape hers had been in. All she was was a flashlight, streaming through the pasture. I picked her jacket up where she dropped it, looked ahead to the car.

It was coming so fast.

I started running for Doby Saxon then too. Because I'm the stupidest girl in the world, yeah. Running and screaming no to him.

Neither one of us made it.

When I finally saw Chris again, she was jogging down the center stripe, her breath still ragged and deep, her hair everywhere.

I was standing back about twenty feet from the fence, still in the pasture.

The car that had been coming had never even stopped, just ended up hanging a tire over in the ditch, clipping that first line of mailboxes that always gets knocked down, then straightening back up, slapping ass up the road like it was going to shoot straight up the mountains or something, just blast off into the sky, come down somewhere on the coast maybe.

And Doby, he was in the ditch now.

What he was doing was—he was trying to pick up the pages of that thing he'd thrown at the side of the car when it wouldn't kill him.

It had exploded into the air, was still floating.

I held my hand out for Chris to stop, and she did, never making a sound.

Doby was gathering the pages to himself like they were the most important thing in the world.

And then all the dust in the air started glowing again.

Another car was coming.

I stepped out into the light with him, picked a page up from the grass and walked it over. It was crumbly and old and from a typewriter.

"Your hand's hurt," I told him.

Chris was beside me now, just watching.

Doby took the page from me, looked to the car. It was coming just as fast as the last one, was ahead of about a hundred more cars coming home too, each with a crazy Indian hanging his head out the window, screaming.

"You want to get out of the road now," he said to me.

I looked down to the car with him.

"You do too," I said back, and he pulled his busted lips in tight, sniffed. I pretended not to notice. Him being beat-up was nothing new.

"What is it?" Chris said, the papers.

Doby didn't answer. I looked to the car again—twenty seconds—and shook my head no to him.

I wasn't Malory Sainte, I knew. But somebody had to try.

"Gin..." Chris said, my shirt pinched between her fingers, all her weight on the balls of her feet.

Ten seconds.

Doby Saxon was still just staring straight at me.

"Why—why do you want to do this?" I asked.

"A test," he said right back, nodding to the car, coming so slow but all at once too, "it'll float right through me. I'm not even here," and then the car was on us, the headlights made up of a thousand-million particles, Doby looking into them with his eyes still open, like he really could pass through the car.

At the last possible foot, the car jerked away, all its weight on its front tire like it knew it was an Indian car, knew it was time to start just rolling through the pasture.

Whoever was driving must have had some white in him, though. Enough to keep the car on the road anyway.

But still.

It passed close enough behind me and Chris to sting us with gravel, try to drag us into its air. Chris's flashlight clattered to the asphalt, died.

"Gracie's going to call the cops," I said.

"They're busy." It made Doby smile his stupid smile.

I just stared at him, finally shook my head.

"I'm not going to say anything," I told him.

"You're not supposed to," he said back, and, because I knew I was going to cry, I stared hard at him one last time, trying to say it all just that way, then spun around with Chris, didn't look back until we were in the pasture again.

Doby was bent over in the road, trying to pick up another page.

He came up with Chris's flashlight too.

There were no cars coming in from Butte anymore, just suddenly black for as long as we could see. When we looked back to Doby, he was looking at us, I think, hardly twenty feet away, but it had to be just the idea of us, because we were invisible, two antelope standing so so still.

Finally Doby believed it, pushed the heel of his hand between his eyes for a long time then held that hand up so the gauze could stream away like liquid, or blood, just flowing away from him and away from him.

And then he went to the knocked-flat mailboxes, kicked through the mail, didn't find whatever he wanted. A cigarette probably.

I didn't want to be doing it, but I was stamping each thing he did in my head.

And I wouldn't go out with him if he asked, no, but I'd carry him inside me forever, maybe. Tell my own kids about this boy I used to know who…who—

Beside me, Chris was crying too.

I took her hand again and we started walking home, and I only looked back when Chris stopped me.

Doby was just sitting on the side of the road now, not standing. Waiting for another car to come kill him.

And Chris's flashlight was working again.

All the papers Doby Saxon had been gathering were in his lap, and he was reading in his stupid way, where his lips followed what was on the page. But he was stuck right at the first of it, sounding it out, just saying

Claire—

Last night I saw a light moving to the north of the Agency and reached out to it with my heart, because maybe a crew had come through with their boots wrapped in sheep skin and their clothes dipped in tar, the heads of their hammers muffled with wet bunch grass tied on with more grass that would have to be refashioned after each strike, and this crew what they had done was laid down cross ties and rail, and now the light what it could be was the lantern of an engine, pulling a line of cars. In one of those cars, Claire, you at the window, in the hat your mother's sister gave you at the wedding just because you told her it was a beautiful hat and complimented her features well.

I think of you often, yes.

In my mind you're in that window yet, and I'm standing on the deck in Missouri in the boots you surprised me with, and you're not looking at me because we've already said goodbye a thousand times, and have promised not to say it again.

But I lied, Claire.

And not just to you.

You would not recognize me, I fear.

Like them, I am starving.

Have you received any of my recent posts, I wonder? Yesterday and for two days prior there's been an Indian man smiling at me from the water trough by the horse pens. This is the man I've been reduced to entrusting to deliver my correspondence to the stage.

He knows something, Claire.

He watches me even as I write this.

And no, I have yet to tell you about last Winter. This is because there are not the words. But I lie again. Last Winter is in my chest and in my throat. The truth is that the words to tell it as it happened, to try to hold them in my mouth all at once would be to risk them turning at once to water, so that if I parted my lips to speak they would come pouring out until I was empty of life and hope altogether, and would become but another feature of the landscape, to be reclaimed to the dirt.

And the man is still watching.

The name he gave me at first for himself was Tooth, but I know now that was only his name as a child. According to the histories and assorted notes left by Collins before me, of which this desk is replete, Piegan men have one name as boys, but at a predetermined age or ceremony they earn or select another, or have it selected for them.

The name of the man who is now watching me is Yellow Tail.

I wither.

Please, Claire, if this missive ever finds you, I ask that you not come after me.

I've gone too far, you see.

There is water rising in my throat.

I dare not try to speak anymore.

Your husband,

Fr.

October the 15 of 1884

Claire—

It's been three days since I wrote you last. This morning snow was hanging over the mountains but it's too early. We're not ready for Winter again, and won't be for months. The potatoes have failed again and the antelope become wise to the limited range of the few carbines the men have.

Through part of the afternoon a woman I think is called Smokes in the Evening stood in her blanket facing the mountains. It was as if she were standing watch. Or as if she were haunted. We all are.

The first thing I see upon waking is my own breath, rising white before my face.

The Piegan have a word for this, I'm sure, but Collins has failed to record it for me.

I loathe him more each day.

After a year now I finally know why I was awarded this post, I think, and can speak it to you plainly, if you'll excuse the coarseness. I wasn't posted here to institute new policy or to enforce existing policy, thus easing the inevitable transition of which we spoke. Nor was I posted here simply to clean up the considerable mess Collins has left for me, which is both political and pecuniary in nature, and possibly criminal in effect. No, the reason I was advanced to this position so suddenly was because the Commission understood that the situation was unsalvageable.

They mean for me to have been the one responsible, Claire. For twenty years of mismanagement. It's my name the Commissioner will invoke for the next Agent, until Dalimpere will have become, on this reservation, a curse of sorts, a name that you spit from your mouth and then turn away from.

There's nothing I can do to arrest this, either. The time to act would have been when the Deputy Commissioner first requested our attendance at his dinner and regaled us with hide robes and painted vistas and Christian duty.

So now we hitch our blankets tight around our shoulders, in preparation, and we all look west with Smokes in the Evening, and dare not look away until she does.

Would that our blankets were made of meat, Claire.

All the cottonwoods for miles up and down Badger Creek are naked, their bark chewed off early last February by the Indians. The stove wood I write this letter by, even, it's been looted from the stalls, when I thought I was alone.

But then Yellow Tail was watching me.

Standing there with the staves by my leg, I called out to him that it was the federal government's, that I could do with it as I pleased.

His eyes are watery and pale, his smile too casual.

As he's a Small Robe, he should have been dead twice now—once at that slow bend in the Marias, where you can still see the brass shining from the gravel, and once last Winter.

Or perhaps he is dead twice over, and so am I, once from punishment and once in trade, by my own hand, and all that's left for us to do now is to watch over each other.

It would explain why none of your letters have found me.

Unless of course none of mine are finding you.

But I make this posting sound more bleak than is fair.

The Montana scenery is as Edenic as the Deputy Commissioner promised, and the air has in fact been good for my lungs, and once I've seen a herd of not less than thirty elk moving like smoke across the grass, without sound. At first I thought they were buffalo, Claire, that I was going to get to see them like you wanted, for both of us, and for the ears of our five (right?) children, but the only buffalo I've seen as of yet have been crudely painted on the sides of lodges. In remembrance, possibly. Or to lure them back.

Two days ago, on the threshold of the door when I first opened it in the morning, was a fish, Claire. It was the kind of trout that thrives in the mountains, I believe. No kind I'm familiar with, any way.

For a long time we regarded each other, this dead fish and I, and when I came back from visiting with Charles about the deplorable state of the school, for which I also blame Collins and his predecessors, the fish remained.

I packed it in the dusty snow that's not really snow yet, with the intent of giving it as a gift, perhaps. Possibly it could even be interpreted as a sign. But then last night I woke ravenous, and slit the frost from the fish's already slit belly, and stoked the fire in order to sear the meat.

And then I understood why this fish had been left.

Inside, lodged in the stomach, which had been left, was the denuded knuckle bone of a man. Or woman.

What kind of sign is this supposed to be, Claire?

My face grew in turns hot then cold, and my breath came unevenly, but finally I succumbed to the baser needs and ate the meat of that fish until my beard was oily with its grease.

The knuckle bone I interred in the belly of the stove.

A month hence, it will be ash.

And I wish I could tell you that it made me ill, Claire, that I'm still of that quality of man whose body will reject what the man knows to be unnatural, but when I cracked the door open this morning, I did so carefully, in case there was another fish waiting for me.

Given enough of them, and from the same stream or pool, I could reconstruct a whole man in my stove, possibly, and then hold discussions with him. Talk policy. Tell him about you, so that he could feel a pity for my situation that I can't decently ask of anybody on this reservation, nor honestly (I know) expect.

But still I feel it, Claire.

The absence of you, the resulting incompleteness of myself. I should never have left your embrace. I should never have left you, alone.

Has something befallen you, perhaps? Cholera, or violence? Fire, flood? Have you been caught in some labor uprising, or are you currently bartering your way onto a wagon train out here, or is it just a new suitor that keeps you from writing, or is it that you do not recognize my hand in this mechanical type and think it a charade? Has your father convinced you that I've run away to the West, or are you waiting as I am here, each thinking only of the safety and happiness of the other?

This letter, if you get it, means that my new means of posting my correspondence has been a success.

If, however, it doesn't, then, Yellow Tail, if you can follow my hand, know that in his indirect, shuffling ways, Marsh has told me about your wife, whom he refused to name.

From the notes Agent Collins left, however, I know what that means.

My condolences.

Fr. Dalimpere
Indian Agent for the Blackfeet
1884

Claire, Claire Dalimpere—

Your name like a song. If that indeed is what you still call yourself.

But I allow myself liberties of imagination, as if I want the pain of this separation in lieu of any word, as it can at least serve as a connection.

Rather, if I'm to dwell, I should nurture the memory not of our wedding day, though it was grand, and not of the first time we met formally, though I could still count each stone of your aunt's court yard, and do, but instead that afternoon we hired a cab to take us through the city to see, if we could, on impulse, a dogwood in bloom. How we were alone in that painted carriage, in the middle of life, you and I, the sides of our hands in constant contact because your aunt wasn't there (our hands below the window, of course). How afternoon lapsed into evening and another driver leaned over to light our driver's lanterns for us, and he did the same for that other driver in return, and we moved through it all in wonder, afraid even to speak lest we perturb the perfect illusion, as if it were a fragile image on the surface of a pond and could ripple away if we but breathed in too reckless a fashion.

But we couldn't help breathing hard either, and I've never prayed so fervently not to find a tree in bloom, nor had to apply myself so earnestly not to crack my voice when we finally did and our driver threaded one of the sleeping blooms through your hair and promised us it would open with the sun, if we could stay awake that long, and, he winked, out doors, a wink I only remember now, as the sun boils up out of the grass.

Montana is too far from it though, I fear.

Its heat will never get here.

I'm going out on rounds now, or that's what I've recorded in the log, in case I don't return.

I won't lie to you though, Claire.

In my inner pocket, because paper is too delicate to last the Winter, is the base of a switch like the Piegan men will use to count.

The notches on my stick will be for the living.

I will cut those notches deep.

your loving,
Francis
21 d'octobre

Claire—

Use this as currency if you will. You have only to show it to an ethnographer at the museum, and then I should think you would be able to name your price.

Two days into my count—I was riding north and east, as if a looping counter clockwise circuit might be the secret form with which I could requisition another month or two— I encountered a Piegan boy of about twelve years old. But encountered does not do the experience justice. The truth of it is I was drawn to him, Claire. On this whole sea of grass which is northern Montana, he was the only other motion besides myself and my horse.

It was what he was doing that fascinated me.

At first I didn't understand.

Was he trying to teach a bird to fly, perhaps? Had an elder fashioned for him some aerodynamical toy as yet unseen by white man?

But then I understood, and placed a palm on my horse's neck. Just to feel the warmth there, I think.

What the boy was doing was killing himself.

From some fire pit or stream bed he had scavenged a smooth black stone the size of a cat's head.

He never saw me either, or if he did thought perhaps only that I was the white man come to get him, to collect him when he was done with what he was doing. That the

Winter snow swirling to our west had taken form, saddled a horse and finally stepped out into the grasslands to punish his people. Starting with him.

Did he think he was a sacrifice?

I like to think so, yes.

But he wore none of the paints the Piegan associate with ceremony. And, this I would only see later, upon closer inspection, he was crying as well. Afraid. But still, time and again, he would lower the stone down to the top of the grass in both hands, his knees bent to either side, and then hurl the stone as high into the sky as he could, less as if throwing it, more as if simply releasing it.

And then he would watch it until it broke over for the ground, and he would try to line it up with his head.

We will never understand the Indian mind, Claire. No Commissioner or ethnographer or Indian Agent will ever be able to write it down into a book in any complete fashion.

Three times I watched that black stone hang in the air, a speck against the blue, and then plummet down, that boy running for it, leaning into it as if to catch, only he led with his head.

The first time the stone glanced off the point of his right shoulder. He dropped like a sack of onions and lay there for long moments, but then rose and threw the stone with his left arm but it flew wide, too far for him to run under.

The third time, however, the stone pulled itself into the sky as if on a vertical string, and then rode that string back down to that boy's waiting face.

At the last instant, and you can't blame him for this, he turned away, so it caught him in the vicinity of the ear.

But it was enough.

Again he dropped.

For a long time then I just sat my horse, my wrists crossed over the pommel, my breath coming in gasps I would admit to no one but you, and finally a figure resolved on the rise opposite me, so that I had to look across the body of the boy to see who it was.

Yellow Tail.

As is his custom, he was dressed in layers of cast off cavalry uniforms and tied together hide.

We didn't raise our arms to each other either, Claire.

Instead, we stood witness to this, mute.

But then, and this isn't for the museum, Claire, but for you alone, so tear the paper where appropriate (I pretend you're in need of cash, you see. It helps to explain your silence), the boy stirred, such that blood poured from his mouth into the soil, and it was like the Winter past was welling up all around me again.

I spurred my horse down to him, was cradling his head in my lap by the time Yellow Tail arrived, his eyes never leaving mine, as if searching for a response.

In my saddlebags was jerky and pan bread, nothing.

I had yet to even make a notch in my willow switch, thinking I would count all the Indians camped in Badger Valley upon my return, as the cold would be pushing more of them in by then, thus inflating their numbers and reducing the perceived toll of last Winter, and, thus, my spiritual debt to the Piegan.

But Yellow Tail of course could know none of this.

What I said to him, my words jammed together with an urgency I don't remember ever having expressed, was that we needed medical provisions, and water, and shelter.

What he said back was articulate and winding and lyrical, but no more intelligible than the liquid sound of a brook.

And then I laughed, Claire, laughed at the futility of it all and looked away, closed my eyes but couldn't stop my chest from heaving, and finally looked up again to Yellow Tail, cursing him roundly, using my hands to show him what I needed.

Again his response was guttural and meaningless.

And then the boy's foot jerked, on the puppet strings of some long muscle buried in his leg, and I pulled his head tighter to me, so that I was bent over him, and close, so that only he would hear when I promised him that if it could at all be in my power, then he would live. That I would find a way to save at least one of them, even if I had to shave the meat from my own ribs.

It was stupid and impulsive and vain, I know, and over-steps any number of boundaries I'm supposed to maintain as Agent for these Blackfeet, Claire, but, as a man, as your man, your husband, could I do anything else? Separated for so long from you, I think what I wanted was to become a good enough person to earn your presence again. It was a test, I mean, not of my federal duty, which has less and less sway this far from the Commissioner's offices, but of my essential Christian nature.

But as I said, it was hardly selfless. Perhaps admitting to that here will ameliorate the ballast of my sins in some small measure. Except I no longer even trust myself enough to guarantee that that in itself is not part of a deeper charade. So let me just say it. If I could save that boy, Claire, I believed that the world would have to tip in my favor finally, such that you would slide down it and into my arms, safe.

And it was poor judgment, and I was simply not de-signed for the job I've been assigned to, my temperament was not and is not and never will be sufficient for it, but, too—did you know that the Piegan believe that the utterance of words is not always just a description of the world, but that, in certain circumstances, be they ritual or incidental, those words become the thing itself almost, and thusly impinge upon the world in ways civilized man has no longer any conception of?

What I'm saying, Claire, is that the boy, at the time of my writing this entreaty to you, he lives yet.

My promise, my barter, my appeal, it impinged upon the world.

I will, I know now, see you again, sit by you again, the sides of our hands touching in modest advance of our eyes.

As for the unexpected mechanics of his survival, the hour is late and the flame it gutters and coughs and I have not the resolve right now to tear any more wood from the stalls, so let the rest wait for another night.

Aslumber,
Fr.

Claire—

I have not written a report for Sheffield now in two weeks. My hope is that my apparent ineptitude will force him to replace me with some one more capable, whose tenure the Commission will have to bolster with a full delivery of rations.

The first snow has fallen, yes, and our hearts with it.

For me, now, everything depends upon the boy. His name, as near as I can translate it for you, is Lead Feather.

And yes, Sheffield, I finished rounds after attending to him, though he did initially slow me by a full three days. The rest of the circuit went twice as fast as usual, however, and has resulted in the most comprehensive count yet, I feel. This time, you see, I had an invested guide, one who knows the contours and byways of this reservation as you or I might be familiar with the ridges that roove our mouths. We could not draw them, no, nor mold them from clay, but have an awareness of them more intimate and unthinking than any other.

This is how Yellow Tail moves across his ancestral land. Each coulee informs him of the presence of the next, and the story of each of them, which way a deer might run for shelter or how many mounted warriors each could, and has, held. It's a spiritual geography, such that distinctions between him and it, the land, at times fall away.

All of which is to say yes, we speak to each other now.

This is how it happened. With the boy Lead Feather's bloodied head in my hands as if I'd committed the crime myself, I whispered my promise urgently to him, so urgently that my position as ambassador of the American government momentarily slipped, and I spoke as you and I do, when it's imperative your aunt not follow.

You remember maintenant, ça?

French, Claire. My father's French.

In it, over the cooling body of Lead Feather, Yellow Tail asked me back if my promise was real or if it was just like all the rest?

I looked up to him as if seeing him for the first time, and nodded once, yes.

His French is easily as good as mine.

As a boy, evidently, when he was still Tooth and not yet a man, he had been sent to live with a pair of French trappers at their Winter camp. His mission had been to show them where the beaver and ermine and muskrat and hare were, as surely once the trappers collected their fill, they would pack up and leave, right?

Paramount to that, too, under no circumstances was he to let either of the trappers die, as they were far enough from their home that their spirits would be caught out here for generations, scaring the game and bringing sickness and bad luck.

This becomes the story of how he earned his name, Claire. How he became a Piegan man. And more.

At the end of that Winter, which was trying to reach the beginning of the next Winter, so that the snow would never melt but persist in all the places hidden from the sun, he sneaked back to his band's low camp and found his people cold, all the fat gone from their bodies, their eyes hollow and saturated with smoke.

The next night he returned to the circle of lodges pulling behind him a mountainous sledge of furs.

Behind him, not buried in trees but in the snow, lay the two French trappers. In life they'd been dirty enough that when they had to relieve themselves in the night, they had just done it in bared feet from the flap of their lodge. This served to stain one side of their pallet of furs, which, once the furs were unpacked and thawed, turned out to be the tails of most of the animals. Thus the name.

We can smile at the random justice of it, Claire, but Dalimpere is no more intentional, as I'm sure you know.

When Yellow Tail told me this story, he framed it as just another of his wandering humorous interludes meant merely to pass the miles and distract me from my sworn duty, but I can follow it to its conclusion too.

It was an introduction, an explanation, what in savage terms would have to amount to a confession.

You see, his wife succumbing with the rest last Winter, the Small Robes being massacred nearly twenty five years ago, the Piegan's ancestral lands dwindling until the buffalo all went to sleep in their secret cave, Yellow Tail heaps this all upon himself, Claire. For killing those French trappers. For having kept his people warm.

It's left him a pariah, a fish eater who lives in the mountains alone with his not inconsiderable grief.

Until I drew him down, that is, just as the boy with his stone drew me.

I feel he has a plan for me, Claire, Yellow Tail. And I can no more see it than I can count the grains of snow as yet filling the hollow places of the reservation.

Fr.
10 novembre

My dearest Claire—

I have yet to tell you about the dreams. Maybe in a subsequent letter.

This morning a post arrived from Sheffield. It was filled with invective and laced with menace and threatens to indict me in a federal court for my November actions, with which he claims no complicity. I would expect no less.

Now that Winter is here, Yellow Tail some times leaves for two days at a time with no explanation.

Other days we ride together to see to Lead Feather. He sleeps still, if you can call it sleep and not breathing death, in the wallowed corner of his family's dugout. His father, I believe, is the one called Catches Weasel. I don't know whether Lead Feather is the boy's boy name or his Piegan name either, and feel it rude to ask, when his survival is as yet unguaranteed.

In one of the days Yellow Tail was gone I sifted the knuckle bone from the ashes of the stove and deposited it in a supple leather bag I found in a locked cabinet. All it had in it was ash and crumbled leaf or tobacco and half of a chert arrowhead with a vein of red shot through it and an unfired lead slug of the kind that requires an unrifled barrel. Yellow Tail says the bag is the scrotum of a buffalo bull in his second year. Someday it will be a curiosity in my library. For now, however, what it has in it aside from the arrowhead is an unclaimed knuckle bone and a glass bead I found outside a lodge last summer and the bottom plug of the willow switch, which I cut off on accident, trying to notch Lead Feather's life into it deeper and deeper.

If I can just save one, Claire.

He won't make up for the rest, no. But if he dies, I fear the added weight of him will tip the rest over and they'll come piling down upon me, such that I can never climb out again and will have instead to drown in what I've done.

And I should be recording for you the stories Yellow Tail recites, as they will surely die with him, but they are so many and so diverse and unconnected until six nights later, if even then, and half of them seem to be meant as jokes. Should I tell you the story of the ducks and berries, that I think was meant as a lesson in spite of how it sounded in French, or would you rather have me recount his mystical disorientation in the mountains in the days after Marias, when he was shot twice through the leg and dying, able to speak to animals, or would you rather I repeat the obvious lie that his name doesn't derive from those French trappers' urinary inclinations at all but from a mountain stream he once sat in to cure an unmentionable malady, a stream which, when he stood, was swirling with flakes of gold?

My nights are not lonely anymore any way, or peopled with my unfettered, fear impelled imagination, and for that I'm grateful. And some times Yellow Tail will even let me speak. I've told him about the dogwood, Claire, tried to make it real for him though there are no ornamental plants out here, and I've told him about my brother's Jesuit classmates at the wedding and what they did in jest, which your father didn't see the humor of, and in turn he's told me about his passed wife, whose angular face and black spill of hair I think I might remember from last Winter, as one of the last ones to have succumbed.

Even so, she was buried with the rest on the rise west of the Agency, but first had to lie there all Winter like cord wood.

By my rude count, and including Lead Feather, the Piegan numbers were nearly halved last Winter, after they'd already been halved by pox.

You can almost understand a young boy lofting a stone into the air and then not looking away, can't you, Claire? Or perhaps I'm giving in to the same despair. Perhaps, if species personality or cultural attitude is in fact defined by the land one is immersed in, then I'm merely exhibiting what any sane person would in similar circumstances.

Either that or I'm

Nothing.

I will write you again anon, when Yellow Tail has sneaked out. Even now I think he stares at these letters to you as I sleep, or pretend to sleep. And it's not as if I'm even addressing them anymore.

As ever, your
Francis
novembre 1884

C—

You have become a figment. I could carve you from green wood and enshrine you in a cut bank in the creek and bow my head to you in supplication and it would be the same as now.

Forgive me.

Fr.
1883, 1884, 188–

For the honorable Claire Dalimpere—

I regret to inform you that your husband, Indian Agent for the Blackfeet Indian Tribe of Northern Montana, has succumbed.

Taking heed of his postal silence, my men duly trekked to his Badger Creek post.

The Pikuni were standing in a loose circle around the disrepaired Agency grounds, each facing in, their faces typically unexpressive.

In the middle of the circle, and I have to assume you would want to know this, your husband. He was in his long underwear, his face bent to the lowest slat of the horse pens. He was chewing on that slat. To what end or purpose we have no supposition, but have to assume some form of dementia, perhaps resulting from his extreme isolation or perhaps stemming from the advance repercussions of his inevitable trial and sentencing.

You see, last Winter, for reasons only he could have related in full, he apparently stood in the back of an Indian council until he was permitted to speak.

First, however, he unshouldered the blanket he had tied into a sack. In it were all the provisions the Agency was stocked with, including even the coffee and tobacco and salt.

The provisions rolled from the bag and stopped, and no

Indian in attendance reached for them, though each could have told you the position of every last tin.

What your husband said then, Mrs. Dalimpere, we have only inexactly, from the one they call Marsh, who tends the Agency grounds and, according to him, the mail as well in recent weeks. However your husband said it, though, it was a crime, from which guilt he's now retreated to the hidden recesses of his interior self.

As I'm sure you know, the Pikuni gain revenue by leasing their unused land for grazing. It's a profitable situation for them, one which both keeps the land from going to waste and should provide for them for perpetuity. And, though of course the ranchers who lease that land are all Montana citizens, some of them have contracts to provide the United States military with beef. But I overcomplicate the matter. Such are the ungentle ways one becomes accustomed to, living in the company solely of men. Suffice it to say that these cattle which are promised to the cavalry are considered by the government to be federal cattle. Thus, dispensing with them is an act wholly under control of the government through its officials. Of which your husband, though in remote and tenuous service to the Indian Commission, is never the less not included.

His 'herd,' if you will, is human. More or less.

So when he stood at the back of that council and told these Indians to go out onto the Winter plains and harvest whatever cattle their penury and lack of foresight had made necessary, he was authorizing the destruction of property over which he had no jurisdiction, and in effect taking meat from soldiers' packs. In ruder times, an individual committing an act such as this would simply have been hanged, as you know. But civilization has come to the West, Mrs.

Dalimpere. Now we require a public trial.

And, lest you allow yourself to think that your husband's betrayal of his own kind resulted in saving the life of an Indian or two, know this: first, that they breed and live like dogs, second, that one or two doesn't matter, as they fail to feel the loss of a family member in the same way we might, or even recognize proper familial relations, and, lastly, if my man is reading the notes scattered around the Agency correctly, then nearly six hundred Pikuni died the Winter hence and were buried in a single grave.

What could a beeve or two have even done, do you think?

Rather you should throw lit matches at the coming Winter.

Tragedies abound out here, Mrs. Dalimpere. I only apologize that now we must count your husband as one more. And, as for the Pikuni to whom he was supposed to be bringing agriculture and prosperity in the name of the United States government, even when no treaty specifies such a burden, know that their loyalty lasts only as long as the rations. As we dragged your husband away by the scruff of his neck, only one of the standing Pikuni remained.

When my men called out to him he answered only in bastard French, and when we came back to the stalls again he was gone. In his place, balanced atop one of the posts, was a smooth black rock about the size of a grown man's hand.

We left it there,
Claire
Claire Dalimpere
With a flower in her hair.
God.

And I say that in supplication only.

In apology for this,
which you'll never receive any way,
nor remit,
Francis, your husband
14 novembre

Claire—

Something is happening, of a scope I am not prepared for.

Yellow Tail is not what he seems.

His jokes are true and the stories he tells of things that happened as little as two years ago patently false.

I leave you this only as a record, should you or your father feel duty bound to come out here to try to piece together what has happened to me. I keep these missives to you rolled tightly in a burlap sack in the hollow post of the frame to my bed, though it's a futile gesture, for Yellow Tail will, I know, find anything I hope to hide, no matter if I eat it even, and thus will I be disappeared, erased from all human history.

But perhaps that itself is contingent upon Lead Father.

More and more I feel like he is the hinge upon which the world up here turns. As if the land could take the insult of last Winter, it could swallow five hundred and sixty five Piegan, but it can not or will not open to receive this one more boy. Or if it does, there will be repercussions.

Catches Weasel raises his hand now when I appear on the second rise distant from his dugout, which I believe has been reclaimed from a military bivouac of some sort. There are circles in the ground around his dugout, the soil there noticeably darker. Yellow Tail says that's what happens when wood rots for many snows. Their configuration and distribution cause me to think that wood was horse stakes.

Possibly, a hundred or two hundred years ago, before the Piegan even had horses, a lone explorer walked away from his company or military detachment and opened his notebook and tried to record some of what he probably considered majesty.

I know better, though.

That beauty is a trap.

Though Yellow Tail can not decipher English, he can nevertheless read this on my face, I think. For it makes him smile, and adjust his stories accordingly, telling me how to survive in the snow should I ever find myself alone and bereft in it, and what animals are prone to harbor you in such a situation. But he could be giving me a manual for suicide as well.

Some nights I breathe hard, for no apparent reason at all. Other nights I watch my breath rise and pray for Lead Feather.

The world on him depends.

Without him, I'll never see you again.

If anything else matters, I could not name it.

Still Novembering,
Fr.

My Claire—

I think it has to do with the two French trappers. Perhaps Yellow Tail intends for me to ferry them back to their own kind, on a raft made of myself. This is why he stretches me thin with lies and smiles and stories of how the guns sounded twenty four years ago in his ears. Or perhaps he has returned to their snowy graves and plundered their bones, and grinds them now into the pemmican he some times shares. Perhaps he doesn't even have any children. They're where he says he is when he's not at the Agency. According to Marsh, Yellow Tail has fourteen sons, each stamped from a different time when it was more difficult to die, but I trust Marsh no more. Yesterday I thought I saw a dent in his head like the one Lead Feather will surely wear, and immediately I knew that this was a world I had created on my own, and ran my hand over the top slat of the stalls. Just to keep my mouth off it, yes. I no longer know what drives me, and the questions Yellow Tail asks in his sly, childlike voice, I can not tell whether they're mere savage conjecture meant to probe the white man's mind or whether there's a more devious point to all this.

Again I start to think I died last Winter after offering my food to the council, that I starved in the Agency house alone and the Commission sent no replacement, because all the Piegan died as well, and now I move among them on their unfamiliar ghost roads as the two French trappers surely must, unaware of my own demise, simply creating problems to continue fooling myself that life yet persists.

Just a word from you, Claire, and I would know I am alive, that I am not just the white spectre in Lead Feather's extended dreams. Perhaps that is why it is imperative that he wakes. Or that you, to me, do.

But your face, though it grows no bit dim in my memory, it is yet frozen.

You're probably an entire different person by now, who needs not a marooned Indian Agent, one who does not even need himself.

I haven't told you that in the summer months Sheffield informed me of the pending suit against me, for my shameful crimes of last Winter. And that I should be wary in the coming months of compounding them.

Yet the rations for December, am I to think they're on the way?

One of the stories Yellow Tail tells me, as a dare I think, is that his horse is enchanted. It's neither fast nor picturesque nor of a stature or temperament or coloring that you would want to breed into another line and thus preserve, but still, you can take your knife and cut from its flank a steak or two every few days without killing it, and the horse will feel no insult, no injury, provided you pack the wound with the proper paste and blow smoke over it in thanks.

After telling me this, Yellow Tail smiled and offered me his own blackened blade, asked if I was hungry?

Twice now he's brought fish to my table, pulled from some lake or stream unseen by any white man.

There were no bones in them but fish bones.

Francis

C—

This is in haste, so needs must be brief. The storm comes, you see. Smokes in the Evening no longer stands guard against it, holding it back with her stare, which tells it in no unyielding terms that it is to be held accountable for her four sons and two daughters, and her husband now gone worthless with grief and self destruction. Perhaps in order to survive this Winter she has donned some town woman's bonnet and hoop skirts, as coldness and hunger would seem to only be an Indian affliction.

I no longer wear the suit you last saw me in. It no longer exists.

I write this as final goodbye, possibly.

I am going to Catches Weasel's.

Yellow Tail claims he could find it in any weather, and I believe him, for he seems invested in Lead Feather as much as I. But before we can leave he has to move among the lodges circled down from the Agency to beg me another horse, as mine was gone from the stall when we went to retrieve it. Perhaps it too is running in advance of the storm. By now those lodges Yellow Tail moves among must be invisible, however, even their smoke pulled away. But we must make it to Catches Weasel's. And this is punishment, I know, and not unjust. The wood I have been looting from the Agency stalls has weakened those stalls. I am the one with no foresight, Claire. Clair.

Clare. If I spell your name in every way will that force the world to give you to me, or will it make it seem I'm a stranger who doesn't deserve you, an admirer who has never received a missive from you in all this time and thus knows not the letters that make you up? I do not know if when Yellow Tail returns I will roll this into the leg post of my bed with the rest or if I will tuck them all into my shirt as if hiding them, or saving them to burn in private. Perhaps it will be better that they go unfound. It will make it easier for you to move on as you must. There will be no record to dispute what your father will surely be telling you about me. And assuredly he is right, Claire. I was wrong to ever leave you. I feel it more every day, every night. This is not my country. If I die out here the land will inter my bones but my soul, Claire…I do not know. Yellow Tail has polluted my thoughts. He's noticed the leather bag I carry on my belt, and thinks it embarrassing for me, that I'm trying to have medicine like him, that I would rather be Indian than Indian Agent, that, like the young men of his tribe, I must needs go on a mountain fast to acquire my second, true name. But I would not wish that, Claire, unless starving myself in such a lonely fashion could hasten my return to you, or you to me.

Would our children have had grey eyes like yours, do you think, or would they be tow headed like me, and foolish, inclined to romance? Would they ever find the willow plug my younger self once tried to save an Indian boy's life with, and know my lie when I said it was nothing, a mere souvenir? But that French word would bring it all rushing back, too. This. All of it. And I would cry in my study until you stood at the door and asked me if it was snowing again, if I was still walking through that snow to Catches Weasel's, and I would nod and sob yes, it was so cold, yes, and and and I try only to say it in such a way as to put it behind me already, as something accomplished, when in truth it is a two day ride in fair weather, on a horse fat with Agency oat and familiar with both my weight and the journey.

Each time I go now to the window I think I see Yellow Tail taking form through the skirls, leading two horses by the bridle, but it's only sailor's fancy. I know because I've seen the dead from last Winter as well, standing in a circle around the Agency grounds, no longer pervious to the cold. They wait for me to eat the Agency house, and the office itself, and the school and the store room and the outbuilding the rations once festered in and every other article and relic of the government's presence on their land. And I would, I think, Claire. I would. But instead my lot is to tend the boy called Lead Feather, because it was providence that allowed me to see him in the first place. My lot is to pray for him to my God and to his god and to gods as yet unnamed but created in the act of my praying. To walk out into the storm when Yellow Tail returns and holds the hackamore over to me, the wind too harsh even for words. And even though I describe him with as much force as I can, still, my descriptions do not cause him to have come back with a mount, so I sit here with your name on my lips and the souvenir of your hand touching mine in the back of that carriage and I want to include with this the pages I've been secreting away even deeper in my bed post, because maybe my lies of exclusion have become the wall between us, or around me any way, and thus I need to tell you not just what I think is fit to hear or that which I think won't drive you away but the aspects of these last few nights which defy explanation and cause me to question the true effects of grief and isolation and guilt. Whether what I've started to see in my sleep and suspect in my waking is figment or memory. In the midst of it, I do not even recognize myself.

The wall is crumbling, Claire.

Yellow Tail is there through the snow, I think, a small impossible form against all that white.

I go now to join him.

I write this from the field of my first federal posting.

It is my fourteenth month without you.

Unless of course this and not the other is my dream. In which case I've made you up solely from whisper and longing, which I must at some time have expressed in my sleep, save that Yellow Tail has found an English reader for these letters.

That he is to blame, however, of that there can be no doubt.

All that remains in question is whether he does this for purpose or for amusement, or as prelude to this journey before us, when, as last night in my dream, I will be walking behind him through the snow, so that all I can see is his back.

For steps at a time it's gone and you almost fall asleep, but then the wind wraps around as if breathing in, so the air just hangs there, the flecks suddenly suspended, swirling, waiting for you to see that dark brown form, never looking back but never pulling too far ahead either.

Promising yourself again that this is the last time, that you can't possibly take another step, you shove yourself forward, lean downhill, one numb foot after the other. Not because you want to live but because you want to open your eyes, have this all go away, be a joke you've been playing on yourself.

As for how long you've been walking: it's the only thing you remember.

As for who that is in front of you: wasn't your dad's coat red and grey? But who else could it be.

As for the horses, they're gone, something bad.

But—not horses.

Why would you think *horses*?

It's snowmobiles. Now you remember. The *snow*mobiles are crapped out, buried, part of the Park now.

And the elk you jumped yesterday, or the day before that. Whenever. They were monsters, craggly and thick, from back before stupid tags and lotteries, and there'd been so many of them, just flowing up from Two Dog Flat or somewhere, racing like they didn't need any fat at all for the rest of the winter, like they knew some secret warm place for grass, and were almost there now.

By then the first flakes had been falling too, slow and big like a Christmas cartoon, so you had to breathe them off your scope then wait for the cheap-ass lens to unfog. By the time you got the crosshairs settled again though, leading that one second from the front, his horns tilted back along his body like a shield almost, your dad was hooking his head back to ~~the horses~~ the *snow*mobiles.

"What?" you said to him, thumbing the safety forward anyway.

He shook his head no about it, though, your safety.

If this was your first bull ever, then maybe he would have let you blast it. But that first bull's years back already, not even a snapshot in your head anymore, just a story you used to hear him tell, about how the gun kicked you almost all the way out of the truck.

You're glad he doesn't tell it anymore.

But still, this was going to be your first Park elk anyway. Before, it's always been just sneaking them past the wardens. Now there's rangers too. It's supposed to make the meat sweeter.

And you probably should have just gone ahead and pulled the trigger, you know, but by the time you'd half-decided to, your dad was already straddling his snowmobile, his rifle slung behind him, his mouth curled into that smile your mom doesn't like, because it's catching.

"Guess you're waiting for the really big ones, yeah?" you said to him, hissing at the last of the cows streaming into the trees.

This is a back and forth you've heard him use with one of your uncles.

Your dad didn't answer, instead watched the trees the elk just slipped into, like he was making sure, marking their spot, and then he laughed through his nose and you shook your head in disgust, because this wasn't even going to be an argument. He didn't have to say aloud what you could read on his face: that blasting those elk like this, it would be nothing, just a thing for kids or white people. What would be something, though, would be to burn ahead to wherever that herd was running, then pop them as close to the Line as possible. Let them deliver themselves. *That* was the Indian way.

What really sucked about it too was that he was right. If you blasted them down where they were, on the uphill, it would take both snowmobiles to pull even one back to the reservation, and you'd have to do that five or six times at least, with the weather clamping down and the rangers working all the Park roads, swinging the gates shut. And anyway, those racks would leave drag marks in the snow outside the treads, so the rangers would know exactly what had happened here.

If you caught the elk heading for Racine Basin or way back behind Volly's or something, though, then there'd probably be a road close enough to back a truck in.

"Okay then," you said to your dad, pulling your right glove back on, having to bite it to get it all the way up your fingers.

It would be like working the coulees out in Landslide. Like the old days, like real Indians.

Except it wasn't.

You should have blasted those elk right when you saw them. The whole herd. Just knocked them flat down, and kept shooting into them.

Because then you wouldn't be here, asleep on your feet again.

You shake your head until you think you're awake again, finally settle on your dad standing still, his back resolving through this snowglobe you're standing in together.

No matter how long you waver there, too, trying to focus, to be sure, he won't look back. Like it's a rule or something. A deal he's made.

Have you even seen his face today?

Think, think, the slideshow of him flitting through your head, him in the living room, football glowing off his beer-slick eyes, him in a truck pulling away, him standing in the doorway of the kitchen one morning after three days gone, you five years old, suddenly sure he's forgotten who you are, that he doesn't even know what house he's in. Him in the stands at a powwow with your mom, a piece of popcorn low down in his hair that nobody's told him about, not even her. Him standing up on his snowmobile, twisting the throttle back hard to cut the elk off at his secret place, always another secret place, always a better, more perfect place, through some shortcut only he knows about, from *his* dad and all the way back to the bow and arrow days, then him looking back to you, to see if you're coming. And his smile, your mom was right: it is infectious. You feel it spread across your face too—those elk are *yours*—and now you're running for your snowmobile, throttling up higher than you need to and tearing ass after him like this part of the Park's still Blackfeet and you can make all the goddamn noise you want, and if you could have just stopped there, even, instead of earlier, with that second elk in your scope, then maybe—

But he's been standing there with his back to you now for maybe two minutes, waiting for you to take another step, and then ten thousand more after that, each one of them impossible.

When you lurch forward this time, almost falling, reaching to the crust of the snow to catch you, you do it because, for a moment, his head did turn the slightest bit to the left.

It made you realize you don't want him to turn around.

Because of what happened.

If he'd been on a horse, you know, that horse would have sensed the deadfall, floated over it, never looked back.

But the runners of a snowmobile are dead plastic things.

They caught on the deadfall at about forty miles per hour. Fifty if your dad had the throttle all the way open. Sixty if he even had a prayer of cutting those elk off. Seventy to do what it did to him.

When the snowmobile's runners caught, and folded under, stopping all at once, your dad didn't.

At first you thought he was that far ahead of you, that you just couldn't hear him anymore, or that he knew some secret old miners' tunnel through the mountain, or that he'd idled down because the elk were already close, but then—then his...he was—

The rocks.

There was no miners' tunnel. Just the rocks, granite or something, flecked with two different shades of blue. And they didn't care what got thrown against them, at what speed. Sunlight, winter, storms, fathers, whatever.

You pulled him close to you, hard enough to hurt him if he could have hurt anymore, and it didn't matter anymore how much sound you made, and when your snowmobile was just sitting there, its kill switch tied to the handlebars, its runners dumb and plastic too, you pushed your safety forward and shot the tank and the engine and the seat just because the other one was already dead, and then shot them again and again until the magazine was empty, then beat the handlebars with the stock until the rifle was splinters and your snot and tears were frozen all over your face, and

and

now this, somehow. Here. Already.

Blood all over you—he bled that much, even after he was dead?—last night as blank as what you're walking through.

Maybe he was there then too, though. While you slept. Or if. Holding your head to his chest, his back to the wind, his hair frozen into a shroud around his face, a look in his eyes like he always got, like he could do this, like he was *going* to do it whether he could or not, who cared about the fucking rules, and that's where the blood all came from: he was holding you, bleeding, saying over and over again that thing about the .30–06 nearly kicking you out of the truck that first time, and how you hit that goddamn elk anyway, deadcenter. How you're like him, a real Indian.

So you lean forward into the whiteout, step, step again, and are sure now that his jacket wasn't brown like that, even if it is his hair, his shoulders, his walk, and after a few more hours of this you don't even think anymore at all, because all you are is dead, following a ghost, and the dead don't need to think.

Next you're—you don't know where you are. No lights, just an empty sound. Space all around, and dust coating the tile floor, the aftercrash of glass all around you, and display cases. And a name in your mouth, *Dally*, but bleeding back out too, because he had something.

A bat.

He had a baseball bat and he had been waiting for you when you ran out of the…when you ran away from your mom.

That song she'd been singing over your shoulder, in your head, it was her death song. The same one she sang in the hospital, so that anybody or anything listening would know that it was her dying, not you, and so leave you be, let you live.

Only—only if a person lives through singing that, then for the rest of that person's life, she's dead already. All that's left is to figure out how: car wreck, needle, a boot kicking over and over.

And you can't even remember her name, now that you want it. Just her voice, like a ribbon you followed back when you didn't even want to. But she was made of that ribbon, and unwound herself too far, until there was nothing left on the inside.

She won't last another winter. Can't. Not the way she's going.

What you need to do to save her life now is to get her away from all this. From the casino, from the house, from her cousins and sister and brothers and nieces and nephews and friends and enemies, from all of it.

Then her body could stay alive anyway.

After enough years, even, you might could bring her back to the reservation. Because maybe it would have forgotten about her by then. Taken somebody else instead. You, if it wanted.

And that's it.

Of course.

You.

Four years ago, she offered her life for yours. Now it's your turn. Except you don't know any songs for anything. But it doesn't matter. That's the old way. The new way, the way you're making up, is that it's the same if you just say her name right when it happens, the bullet or razor or cliff or windshield or train or however.

It's not like anybody expects you not to, anyway.

The elders already, the way they look through you instead of at you, you might as well be buried in the ground.

But not here, not—not with this glass shattered all around your feet.

Behind you, a metal door frame, a crossbar you didn't have to crawl over because you...because of the bat. You didn't have to crawl over the crossbar because you'd been thrown.

Dally.

He'd been waiting outside the casino, with Luther and Phone and one of the Looks Twices, the little one with the buzzcut.

And the way they were just standing there like a welcoming party.

Had Robbie told them?

No. What had probably happened was they heard the instant legend of your run at the table, and came to cadge a handful of chips, for last weekend.

But now here you were already, no chips.

For maybe five seconds you stood there across from them, until there was no doubt, and then you were feinting one way, crossing over the other way instead.

It didn't matter.

If Dally'd brought the big Looks Twice, you might could have slipped around that side, but the little Looks Twice had been a point guard, and knew which way you were going to cut even before you did.

His knee caught you on the point of the hip, spun you around so that Phone could grab you, slam you sideways into one of the pillars.

After that it was Dally and the bat, a methodical thing where he never really opened up, just kept you down, begging, promising two hundred instead of just forty. Two hundred and your *car*, whenever it got running again.

And that was what he'd been waiting for.

He stopped coming down with the butt of the bat, let you breathe. But then it wasn't enough just to breathe again. Looking straight down at the ground, your own blood stringing to the curb, you felt your mouth curling into a smile, one you'd caught a long time ago and kept hidden all this time.

It made Dally stop, look to Phone to be sure they were seeing the same thing: you, standing when you shouldn't be, trying to think of some good line from a movie. If Dally hits you just right, you can finally remember your mom's name, you know, and say it into the bat, and the trade'll be done, over. Please.

But all you can think for some reason are random words from the two weeks of French you sat through in tenth grade.

Maintenant? Dormir?

And when you try to speak, it's French that comes out.

Dally laughs, says you *are* going to fix that car next week, right?

Because the two hundred, you both know it's a joke.

If you scrape that much together, he won't see you for a week, and that'll just be at the memorial service.

So you keep smiling to him, at him, daring him with your teeth until he spits, wipes his mouth with the back of his hand, says if that's the way it's going to be then, and nods once to Phone.

Phone nods, slams his fist into your stomach high up, and while they're carrying you Looks Twice whispers for you to look his brother up if you need anything. That Indians got to stick together.

At first this doesn't mean anything, but then you remember that the reason you haven't seen the *big* Looks Twice around all this year is that he's down in the state pen.

This is where Dally's taking you.

And the door to it all, it's behind you now, shattered.

You close your eyes, open them again.

The museum. The one that's shut down most of the time now, since the casino opened, like they can't be that close to each other.

Your class came here once in elementary.

But the lights were on then.

You find some of them, the ones for the display cases anyway, and take the tour again, only this time it's not just the same old pipes and skulls and rattles everybody's uncle and grandfather has in the top of their closet or hanging on the wall over their couch. This time the stuff looks *old*. Like you can remember it from when it wasn't. Like that parfleche with the beads, stained down at the corner: you know you've seen that riding around some woman's neck. The old way too, hanging down in the front, not like a purse, where it's just an accessory.

And she was glaring hard at you about something.

You shut your eyes again, tighter, and hold your hands over your face, are breathing too hard now, thinking in French again, only the words still don't mean anything.

What did Dally's bat shake loose?

You lower your head, walk from that room, and there, the lights in the grass shining up at it, is a buffalo.

It stops you.

This.

This is what you—

This is what you've been wanting to see now for years, since you heard the men come back telling of train rides, of plowing through the buffalo on the prairie for three days at a time. Already there's a place in your head shaped for it, waiting for it, another display case, so you can...so you can bring the wonderment back with you. The buffalo. So you can show it to someone else, share it.

You blink it all back, look behind you, to the black and white pictures, the explanations, the sweetgrass braids draped everywhere, and you have to reach out for a wall to keep from falling. But then the wall shatters, was glass. It rains down over the buffalo, the shards lodging in his coat, and without even thinking you step in to sweep them off, see that your hand is coated in blood now, that your blood is glistening on the buffalo's individual hairs, and when you look in front of the buffalo there's a short door to the next display, and you take it too, and now you're in the mock-up of an old time lodge, only there's no smoke like there always is. But still, you don't step between the old man and his fire and whatever he's not saying, just keep your eyes down, looking at the wax holding everything in place, and you know that the people in this lodge are dead now. And that you are too. That you never made it down to East Glacier that time after your dad and the elk, that nobody could have. That—that...

That the cops are going to be here any minute, and that what you have to do to save your mom, you're not going to do it down in the state pen, where nobody can hear you say her name.

It's got to be up here, on Blackfeet land. On land that's *still* Blackfeet land.

So you stand, your hair scratching and catching on the shellacked lodge, and, when the door you try back to the buffalo is locked now, you throw a medicine bundle through the glass of this diorama, follow it out. Because there might be fingerprints on the old leather, you go back to collect the bundle, only when you pick it up it's not from bits of broken glass but from windswept grass.

You're outside.

Because that was a real lodge.

You stepped up through the flap, into the night.

You nod, see the ~~head lanterns~~ head*lights* snaking towards you, and step up onto the blacktop to meet them, waiting till the last blinding instant to whisper the name you've been holding inside, the car so close you think you can feel the hot particles of light on the thin skin at the back of your throat, but then—

It's all a dream, right?

The museum, the snow, this whole life. That's what made it so easy, so natural to step up onto the road like this.

Except now there's the main sound of Indians dying: screaming tires, creaking metal. A stereo pushing one blown speaker out an open window.

It makes you hurt in your throat, and then, an instant later, in your leg or hip, your whole left side, when the mirror or bumper or door bulge or whatever catches you, spins you into the ditch, the stars wheeling, trading places over and over with the grass, like time smearing backwards, and that's it exactly, you know, because now you can remember the rest of it, that Dally's bat only dislodged, and hear what you just said to the headlights, in trade: not *Malory*, like you meant, like it had to be, but

Claire.

For a few steps he'd almost forgotten her name.

When it was his breath, his reason.

Had he fallen asleep again, riding?

No.

He wasn't even riding at all anymore, but sitting.

The wind was turning his outer layers to ribbons, an icy fringe, and if he shifted then the cup of warmth trapped under his arms would slip away, and that was all the warmth he had left.

So he said her name again, inside, and then the snow furnace he was in—that's how he had been thinking of it all morning—shifted, as if in response to a change in the flue, leaving all the white sparks directionless for the moment, just hanging there around him.

It allowed him to see deeper into the storm.

Yellow Tail was gone.

The Indian Agent for the Blackfeet was alone.

He said his wife's name again, like a promise this time, and then the wind cut back through his clothes, pushing the snow into him. He could no longer tell where he ended and the horse began.

Below him, shimmering like candles on the surface of a pond, a spread of lights.

A camp?

With the fires banked *outside* the lodges?

And then he understood.

The Sandhills.

It was where last Winter's dead were supposed to have migrated, where they lived now in their quiet ways, tending the memories of their hunts then boiling that grey meat, chewing it for days, the wind blowing right through them, their fires glowing but cold.

It was how Marsh had explained the breaths of light that sometimes rose from the Ridge where the dead were buried. When he could be made to speak about it at all.

The Indian Agent nodded to himself about this, about seeing this.

It was where Yellow Tail had delivered him, what Yellow Tail had been grooming him for these past weeks. Because penance takes many forms.

The Indian Agent touched his heels to the horse he now had, to go down there, walk among them, but the horse didn't respond. Instead it fell over, to the left, the crust of the snow sheared hard enough that it bloodied one side of the Indian Agent's face, his hands still frozen to the reins, his left leg pinned.

The horse was dead, had been dying all morning. The

best one Yellow Tail could find. For what he intended.

At any moment the spirit of the horse would clamber back up, the Indian Agent knew, with him still astride, and when it snorted, testing the air, its breath would be no warmer than the storm, so there would be no traces of steam, or vapor.

Claire.

What he wanted to tell her was that he was coming home now. That soon he would be able to cross the Dakotas and Missouri and the rest in an unbroken string of days, never having to stop for food or water. That he was going to leave all this behind. That he *could*, that he was still that distinct from it.

He smiled, he was pretty sure, his lips cracking in the cold, and said her name again and again, as if throwing stones ahead of him to step on, and if this was what death was, then—then...

He closed his eyes, had almost thought it: if this was dying, then he had given the Piegan a gift last Winter.

Except he'd seen them in their lodges, their faces drawn, bilious fluid seeping from the rims of their eyes, their hair dull, not a black shroud like an oil painter might render it but a thousand untrackable strands, matted and smoky and tangled.

Had there been a way to boil their hair into broth and live on it for even one day longer, then the Piegan would have taken the knife to their own scalps, the Indian Agent knew. Or had they been able to feed on silence, and resentment. But there was no sustenance in that either. He knew, had tried it, and woke curled around himself in the night, wanting now only to cough it back up.

Instead, what he'd coughed into existence, maybe, was Yellow Tail. At the edge of his vision all through the guilt of spring, just as a pair of eyes, a tobacco-stained smile always accusing, always knowing, but then circling in closer and closer like a wolf or a coyote, finally manifesting across the body of a boy killed by a stone from the sky.

The Indian Agent forced his eyes tighter, tried to remember if he'd ever even seen anyone else interact with Yellow Tail, or if it had only ever been himself.

It would explain why Claire wasn't writing back, he supposed, and then tried to laugh, shook the reins again or meant to anyway.

He'd forgotten how to breathe was the thing.

Standing in the blowing snow now, about six paces out, so that he was just a shadow, a shade, was the bundled, mirthful form of Yellow Tail, one hand hooked in the bridle of his ice-crusted horse.

He was watching the Indian Agent.

Sam.

It was what Yellow Tail had taken to calling the Indian Agent. For no reason the Indian Agent could track. Perhaps just as a form of mockery, to ratify what the Indian Agent already felt about himself, that he had become a stranger to the man he used to be. Or perhaps it was a way of suggesting that Yellow Tail knew that, underneath the Indian Agent's given name, or once untangled from the many intricacies of his station, that Indian Agent was someone else altogether.

That second one, the hidden one, it was the one the Agent had planned on keeping buried upon his return back East. It was the one who had gifted his suit to a young Piegan man of similar build, as the suit was wool, and the snows were starting, and it seemed a kindness, a fitting gesture.

Watching that young man in the dark suit those next few weeks, then, it became a private farce almost, a comedy. How that young man no longer smiled, as he evidently felt the suit more severe than that.

But that was November, a year ago already.

By January, the suit had drifted from Indian to Indian, then become piecemeal. The Agent couldn't help but trace it from lodge to lodge, like a joke gone astray, one he didn't even mean anymore.

The last time he saw it, it was down to just a jacket, the sleeves long enough to cover the hands of the woman wearing it.

She had the pockets stuffed with dry grasses, it looked like. For warmth, perhaps, or for sentimental reasons, or curative ones. Or, by then—this had been early January, if the Winter of 1883 could even be said to have had months— perhaps the grass was going to form the base for some thin, unlikely soup.

The next time he saw the woman, she was dead on the Ridge, the jacket stripped off her narrow shoulders.

He stood over her for as long as he could endure the cold, long enough for the boy tending the dead to pass twice on fingertips and toes. The boy's self-appointed mission was to keep all of their eyes closed, the dead. Otherwise he couldn't sleep, the boy. But he never did anyway, as far as the Agent could tell. Any hour, there he'd be, scuttling from body to body under his calf robe.

Many nights when the Agent locked his door, it wasn't to keep the Piegan from stealing his tins and blankets, but to keep the boy's hands from his own eyes.

Even now, a year later, the Agent had seen the boy standing on the Ridge in the last minutes of daylight, as if he still had work to do there, his fingers dancing on his thigh, perhaps thinking of a bone needle, sinew thread.

And the part of him the Indian Agent wanted to keep buried had seen more, too, more than he'd ever wanted.

Forgotten lodges with the sleeping dead.

Children who had gotten lost in the night.

Dogs feeding on a horse while it was still alive.

A young boy trying to teach a stone to fly.

And now, standing in the skirling snow before him, a ghost, a reflection of the Agent's own guilt and fears and self-pity.

But mostly fear.

Yellow Tail was watching him, and, stacked in a line behind him so perfect as to be invisible, six hundred other Piegan as well.

The Indian Agent nodded about this, that, yes, it was right too. Natural, and painless.

For now anyway.

And then Yellow Tail held out his hand.

Browning.

The word coursed through the Indian Agent, finally came to rest at the back of his throat, like a word he could swallow down if only his eyes would close tight enough.

Was it his wife's maiden name?

Why would he not be able to remember a thing like that?

Was he not going to be able to take the particulars of her down to the Sandhills with him?

He pulled his arm back to himself, and, instead of holding Yellow Tail in his vision, in hopes of keeping him there, solid, the Indian Agent stared along the crust of snow his face was level with and knew in some intimate way that the icy surface was no longer being shaped by the wind but was now giving its contour *to* the wind, to the entire sky, the whole storm.

But then Yellow Tail's hide-wrapped foot crushed down through it.

Above him, a horse breathing.

In his hand, a knife refashioned from some agricultural tool, the pins all filed down, the handle braided over with hide that had been green when wound and since dried hard.

Now, the Indian Agent said to himself, ready to clamber up on his spirit horse's back.

Now, and that Claire's maiden name was French, like his.

And that Yellow Tail, if he even was Yellow Tail, all his blade could be now was mercy. Unless of course the Indian Agent could proffer a trade of sorts. His life in place of the boy Lead Feather's. The Indian Agent taking the Indian's place in the Sandhills, consigning himself to day after count- less day of only knowing the wrong tongue, of not knowing which end of the grey meat is the best, which the worst.

Now, the Indian Agent said again, and raised his chin, giving Yellow Tail his throat, but when the blade didn't come to cut that word out, the *Browning*, the Indian Agent wobbled his head forward again, settled his eyes on Yellow Tail.

With the point of his knife, he was digging into the dead horse's neck, up near the mane.

When the horse didn't respond, couldn't be startled off the Agent's pinned leg, Yellow Tail nodded, wiped the blade beside the pasty gouge and stood, surveyed the storm, finally settled back on the Agent.

In French, he said what the Agent translated as ill fortune, as bad luck.

The word was *maleury*.

Yellow Tail nodded to himself about it, as if the word had given him resolve, and then he unpacked a loosely braided rope from his saddlebag.

Between walls of wind, he tied one end of it to the pommel of his cavalry saddle, the other end around the neck of the Agent's horse, exactly as you would never do with a living horse.

Then, before nodding to his horse, he tried to uncinch the Agent's saddle, but the buckle was too precise for his numb fingers, had too much tension, so he simply cut through it, probably into the horse as well, the Agent thought. Like the story he'd told about after Marias, when an elk had talked to him, had laid down on its side, asked him to weather the cold in his belly where it was warm.

When the cinch gave, the Agent's face rubbed deeper into the snow, and then his own horse jerked, was sloughing steadily away.

Yellow Tail disappeared with it, to reclaim his own horse, already running from the dead thing it was tied to.

The Indian Agent was alone again.

He ran his fingers over his leg for irregularities, but the snow had accommodated him without injury, and on the third try he was able to stand.

Because the direction his horse had been pulled was already broken snow, and downhill, he went that way.

Before he was too many steps gone, though, the Indian Agent looked behind, to his cavity in the snow, to make sure he wasn't there yet.

Marsh.

The Indian Agent nodded to himself.

Marsh. The Dove man who worked the stalls. He had said something about Yellow Tail's dead wife. The one the Agent had, if not killed, then not saved, either.

It didn't matter. Not for this anyway.

If Marsh *knew* of Yellow Tail's wife, then that meant Yellow Tail wasn't a figment.

But of course, too, according to Marsh, the wife was dead, and nameless.

And Yellow Tail?

The same way he had wavered into view across from the boy Lead Feather, now he had taken form across the body of a frozen horse. As if he'd walked up from the encampment of the dead.

Even now he was dragging that horse back there, perhaps to feast on for years.

The Indian Agent staggered to his knees, almost didn't rise again. Could feel the reservation wheeling around him, changing shape so that he nearly had to vomit, or hold his arms to his head and scream against it all.

Whether there was an actual camp down here or merely last Winter's spirits, slouching from lodge to lodge, their sides still drawn, there was no longer anywhere else for the Agent to retreat.

The next time he fell, his knees found rock.

And the next as well.

It didn't hurt, he was too numb for that, but it did jar something awake in him.

A continuous slab of rock out here?

For a few cold moments he tried to brush the snow away with the clubs his hands had become, but it was futile.

Finally he forced himself to stand again, peer sidewise into the wind.

He was in a track still, he could tell between the storm's breathing. Only—it was wider than the one he'd been following. Even if there had been a team, pulling his horse by its paired hooves.

And this track was older too. If it had been made by dragging some implement or outbuilding—for what reason, in this weather?—then that dragging had happened an hour ago or more, so that the surface of the snow only hinted anymore at the pressures that had been applied to it.

The depression was slight enough that the Indian Agent, after staring along it, allowed that he might be organizing it solely in his head, in the seeing. Cobbling together a track from random collections of crests and waves. Because he needed a track, now that Yellow Tail was gone again. Because he needed a direction, even if it was one he made up step by step.

In the storm, any step you take is proof you're alive. Even if you're going nowhere. Or to the Sandhills.

So the Agent centered himself on what he felt to be the slab of rock and let it lead him downhill, aware only in the dimmest of ways of the track he was—not seeing, no. More like remembering. Like his feet would know this route without him.

Whether he was still on rock or just on grass again, he had no idea, and knew better than to try and dig down to see.

He'd already stood up from the snow his allotted number of times, he knew.

The next time he would just stay, tell himself the lie they all do: that he's just going to sit here for a moment. To catch his breath, collect his warmth, reorient himself. Decide on a course of action, a better means of survival. And then fall gently, permanently asleep.

So the Indian Agent for the Blackfeet pushed on, face into the wind, dead on his feet, his eyes set now only to accommodate the dim lights he'd seen from his horse, which, even if they didn't have true heat, would at least have the memory of it, and then at some point in his struggle he remembered a road he'd seen leading out of Boston one February, a road paved with dark stone. The Agent—not an Indian Agent then but just the first one to travel this road that morning—had come around a bend, had looked away from the copse of trees he'd been counting for some reason (Claire: he was meeting Claire's father that morning, to ask for her hand, God) and had seen that the prior night's snowfall, the large flakes he knew had started just after midnight and continued until almost dawn of his sleepless night, that they had blanketed the countryside white and new, only—

There were no fences here, so he shouldn't be able to see the road, should he? Except by the tunnel of trees?

But this was a meadow.

One he knew, granted, and one he had to find if he was to get permission to marry Claire. Except the world was on his side. Claire's father was going to say yes.

The way the Agent had known was that the road before him was clearly visible. Just as much snow had fallen over it as the rest of the meadow, but the paving stones had held onto the heat of the day longer, so that the initial few layers of flakes melted, causing those that followed to rest that much lower.

There was a depression for him to follow.

As now.

Only…only there were no roads on the Blackfeet Reservation. No paving.

Never mind the unforgiving impact his knees had registered.

Or that this depression, this road that wasn't a road but just the memory of one, *his* memory of one, was leading him to the lights he could see now, spread out to either side of him.

Browning.

The encampment of the dead. Of the dead's children, and those children's children.

And they'd been here for more generations than that, the Indian Agent could tell.

Worse still, he belonged among them. Could feel it in the pit of his stomach, the base of his jaw.

He knew this place, had been walking it in his sleep for weeks, stalking it even as he woke, letting it haunt his every movement, as if he could feel it pulling at him, as if it were somehow shaping him, or…or—

Like it already had.

He'd grown up here. Somehow. Knew what was here now and what had been here before.

Claire, he said again.

Not in appeal this time, but in an effort to share this vision with her. With her standing beside him, her hand in his, or even the simplest letter from her tucked into the inner pocket of his jacket, he could make this walk with his back straight, he knew, and damn the rest. He could run the gauntlet of staring dead that had to be lying in wait, who, he already knew, were going to lift their lips in disgust at his awkward presence, that this Indian Agent had followed them even *here*, as if their Sandhills were a federal province now.

And the irregular blocks of shadow he could sense between gusts, or just remember, they were buildings, not lodges. Instead of points, they rose into regular corners. But still, that's all they were, shapes he seemed to remember. To an observer bundled on his horse uphill, upwind so he could look along the thousands of lines of blowing snow, the Indian Agent would simply be stumbling blind through the virgin drifts. Just dying like anybody.

But down here *among* the drifts, down here *in* this encampment of the dead, the buildings, the town, it was here for moments at a time. In the same manner as the depression he was walking in, and taking for a paved road: insubstantial, formed not of brick and mortar and wood and sweat, but of familiarity, of knowledge, of suspicion, of—and not even knowledge, maybe, but *fore*knowledge. Because the blunt shapes he was aware of dimly, knew well enough to avoid, to respect, it was as though they were as yet unborn, save in the Agent's backwards memory—

But he couldn't allow himself these thoughts.

Perhaps they were to the landlocked what the siren was to the sailor. That which lures him closer to the rocks. Closer to the seeming safety of sleep.

As Yellow Tail had engineered, surely.

Because this was a road he himself had already become familiar with? A camp he'd been the hunter for since last Winter, when he followed his wife there? How many other white men had he left shivering at lodge doors? At what smug distance did he now sit, watching, his back to the snow, his mouth not even curled into smile, which made it all worse somehow.

The Indian Agent tried to wipe all this from his face. Tell himself that the wind was blowing no slower down here, that the cold was no less biting. The only real difference was death. With each step, it was both closer and still delayed for another few breaths.

Was 'Sam' supposed to be a way to avoid it, perhaps?

Did the Piegan think they could hide from death under a different name? And, if so, then what kind of kindness was Yellow Tail bestowing, to do it without the Agent's knowledge, or permission, or behest?

If Yellow Tail had in fact ever even been there, the Agent added.

If the Indian Agent hadn't simply freed himself from his horse by cutting the cinch with his own knife. The leather had to have been stiff with cold. It would have given with the slightest breath of pressure.

Now the Indian Agent laughed at himself again.

Browning. The color of sand.

It wasn't that this encampment of the dead was shaping his thoughts, it was the certainty that this particular arrangement of lights and shadows and buildings, it had *always* shaped his thoughts, so that in truth he was a product of it, not the reverse.

Up against that wall a girl had once placed her fingertips to the bones of his wrist during the long moments when his face had been drawing close to hers, to kiss.

But no.

The Indian Agent shook his head no, no: the girl's hair, the girl he remembered, it was inky black, and—and—

Claire, he said aloud, to ward the Piegan girl off.

Claire Claire Claire.

Please.

Claire, Claire, Claire with the yellow hair.

And then he fell to his knees.

Sam.

It was what the Indian Agent was calling himself over and over.

Because his clothes were wet and crackling, his breath ragged, and he had no fire, no horse, no direction save down.

Perhaps, as Yellow Tail had intended, the name was to be his only means of survival. A coward's defense, and maybe that was the final joke: if he became 'Sam,' then would his wife even recognize him, or would he instead become the one keeping his wrist perfectly still under that Indian girl's fingertips, on the chance that that moment could last forever?

The Indian Agent didn't even laugh at himself anymore.

Each building he tried to crouch down by, use as windbreak, would waver and dissipate, the storm blowing through as if it wasn't there at all. And the lights. They were like the lights on the Ridge: spirits, floating in and out of the air, as if threading a line of sinew or cotton back and forth, trying to join the shadow to its source.

But.

The Indian Agent nodded.

The lights on Ghost Ridge.

They weren't ghosts, as Marsh had suggested. No, there was a naturalist's explanation: flammable breaths of gas rising from pockets of decomposing flesh. Because the Indians had been buried in a mass grave. And something about the temperature of the air above that grave?

The Indian Agent shook his head no.

What else could it *be* but spirits?

Of people he himself had caused to starve.

That Sam had caused to starve.

The Indian Agent covered his face with his hands now, but neither his face nor his hands could sense it, so that he spun around, certain that one of the dead was behind him.

He was still alone, though.

In the distance now a pair of spirits in lockstep, pale lights drifting down the way he'd just come, their hands surely joined to keep their bodies so steady.

The Agent watched them long enough to anticipate their path and then scuttled over to what should have been the lee of an adobe building—without meaning to, he could remember its gravel and tar roof, could smell it in the summer heat—turned away as they passed, afraid of catching their eyes, as he might recognize them.

They rushed by in a splash of sound and creaking snow.

The Agent reached for the sill of the boarded-over window, pulled himself up, only realized moments later that the building had been solid enough to do that.

When he went back though, it was shadow again, the wind heedless of it.

He looked ahead, uphill, and kept to the side of the depression he was now calling a road, his hand out to encounter any other wall solid enough to change the course of his arm. But reaching for them only made them retreat, turn to smoke. Yet to stand still was to invite death, to give up, and, even alone, with no witnesses, that might count as a form of suicide, mightn't it?

Was that how Yellow Tail meant to trap him here? By tricking him into damning himself?

Hardly. The Indian Agent had already done that last November, he knew.

He plodded on, past buildings he knew, alleyways he had hidden in, run down, that had been too narrow for…too narrow to be chased down. Other spaces between the buildings he had used simply for shelter, to get—to acquire liquor. And to pass it back out, because, as the notes Collins had left insisted, the Piegan have no real sense of personal property, are not possessed of the proper amount of greed necessary to cultivate civilization. Rather, they gain honor irrationally, by freely giving away their own goods. *Or at least trying to infect others with it,* Collins had added, noting that oftentimes the possessions redistributed had been looted from wagon trains and box cars and plundered homes, where the Piegan had strode over the floorboards, knowing full well the family lay beneath them, holding their breaths.

It was a form of power, Collins insisted. All of it, especially the gift culture.

What had Yellow Tail ever given the Indian Agent, though? Infected him with?

The Indian Agent let his eyes wander over the encampment of the dead, to which he now belonged.

This, he said to himself.

Stories.

Earl.

It was the name Yellow Tail was hiding under.

That and the awning of a faded green wood building with a boarded-over window.

Yellow Tail was sitting there with two other men. Each had their knees to their chests, or close enough, and, between their knees, a bottle in a brown bag.

The Indian Agent made four.

They'd been waiting for him, he was pretty sure.

The one on the end, with the wispy beard, had even leaned forward, said something to Yellow Tail when the Agent sat down.

It was how the Agent knew Yellow Tail was hiding. *Earl* had been the only English word the joking Indian had said.

Yellow Tail hadn't smiled, just slashed his eyes across the road.

The Indian Agent followed, said nothing, for fear Yellow Tail would turn to smoke as well. And then Yellow Tail offered the Agent a pull off the green bottle with the threaded lip, and his eyes, now that the Agent could see them straight on—

Yellow Tail was hiding deep.

If he recognized the Agent, it wasn't with his usual smugness, his usual mixture of tolerance and amusement.

The Agent shook his head no about the bottle, and Yellow Tail reeled it back in to his chest, adjusted his collar against the wind. Settled back into himself and said it again, to himself, as if the Indian Agent's dead horse still wasn't responding to the knife digging beneath its mane, *maleury*, the French word one of the trappers Yellow Tail had been charged with must have used as a curse, or an entreaty.

So at least Yellow Tail's mouth remembered who he was.

The Indian Agent nodded, yes, yes, and grasped Yellow Tail's drinking wrist. *Maleury*, he repeated, holding Yellow Tail's eyes. Poor luck, ill fortune—*this*, being trapped in a storm with one horse between them, and no fire.

Yellow Tail's eyes were empty, though.

The Indian Agent turned away, breathed into the hollow fist of his hand and asked himself what if Yellow Tail hadn't engineered this, but was a victim of the elements as well, and had no more intended to be in this encampment of the dead than the Indian Agent did?

If so, then, unless the Indian Agent could wake him, they were as good as dead. All that remained was the dying part of it.

Again one of the other two Piegan men leaned forward, mumbled something in their guttural tongue, and smiled himself back to the wall.

Yellow Tail nodded, smiled with him.

So he remembered his language, at least.

What else? His nameless wife, his children? Lead Feather?

No.

The massacre. Marias.

Yellow Tail had given it away precisely for this, the Indian Agent told himself. In anticipation of forgetting himself, of losing himself. What he'd done was place his experience in a primitive confabulation and then passed it on so it could return to him someday, wake him from an open-eyed slumber.

The Agent studied Yellow Tail's craggly profile, his oily hair and dark skin, and started speaking in as even a monotone as he could, as if reciting, and the story he relayed was of Yellow Tail bending to the river for a cupped handful of water and feeling the suck of air as the first slug plowed past him, slapping into the water, splintering the smooth rock of the riverbed with such force that Yellow Tail's hand, still cupped under the surface, could feel the pressure as the water absorbed this insult.

And then he was running through the sound, the impossible screaming of the spinning gun, the distinct sound of lead impacting flesh, and in the air there was gunpowder smoke, yes, but there was misted blood and bone too. His family's.

Had two of the cavalry's slugs not burrowed into his leg, he would have cut himself simply from guilt, he knew, and probably been unable to stop.

And he was running yet, climbing, crying, his fingertips raw from pulling, and then the snow—always the snow—it started. He had gone far enough, high enough, that he had come to the snow.

At which point in the story Yellow Tail, *Earl*, lifted his chin west, and up, to confirm what he was hearing here, to anchor the story to the land.

The Indian Agent nodded—yes, there—and went on, trying to recapture the wonder that Yellow Tail had known when he pushed through the last of the trees into that slanted meadow.

Bedded down there, their backs bleached from the Winter sun, was a band of elk.

Instead of running, they regarded him with their large eyes, perhaps wondering how he managed to totter like that, on just two legs.

And then their chief, the one with the horns like the roots of a great upturned tree, he opened his mouth and—

The Indian Agent stopped.

Yellow Tail was awake again. Staring at him intently.

The Indian Agent nodded.

Yellow Tail held his arms up over his head to match what the Indian Agent was doing—massive horns, not just the chief of this elk band but the chief of them all—and the

Indian Agent nodded, unsure why this would catch instead of the rest.

Yellow Tail smiled his slit smile then, turned to the man beside him and said something in Blackfeet, cast his hand to the west, the mountains. Whatever he said made the other Indian's face harden, his eyes go bitter at the corners.

Not Yellow Tail's, though.

The Indian Agent smiled, nodded with Yellow Tail, and then Yellow Tail clapped him on the arm and, moving slow, tracked one of those talking elk across the meadow with a rifle he didn't have, finally bit his lip when he fired, and kept firing, elk plowing chin first into the snow, giving themselves to him.

By degrees he couldn't have measured, the Indian Agent stopped smiling.

Now the man beside Yellow Tail had set his bottle down too, was jutting his chin to the mountains, describing some place half in words, half with the angry lines he cut into the air. He knew this secret meadow where the big elk were, sure, yeah. But it was high, and hidden.

And now Yellow Tail was listening to him instead of the Agent, and soaking it in, turning finally to regard the mountains again then nodding to himself, his eyes losing focus for a moment.

The Indian Agent stood but was invisible to the men on the wall. He held his lips as steady as he could.

If this was another of Yellow Tail's ruses, it was a fatal one. The last one.

Using the smattering of Blackfeet he'd acquired, the Indian Agent farewelled Yellow Tail then, a formal salutation, and Yellow Tail narrowed his eyes at him, and then nothing mattered. The Indian Agent was walking away, across the depression which could be a road or could be nothing at all.

Behind him either the men and their green building remained or they didn't. Either way they were laughing at the Indian Agent. As always.

Twenty paces out, the wind had him again, was blowing through him so that he was sure he was smoke now too, yet still dumbly clinging to the last sensation he'd owned: cold.

Claire, he said, determined to let her be the last breath to pass his lips, Claire Dalimpere. And then he did stop.

Dalimpere.

French.

He had been talking to Yellow Tail with English words, not the French they'd agreed upon. He was supposed to have been relaying the story back to him in *French*.

Other wise he would have been saying nothing.

And of course by now, the men, the green building, that whole side of the street, it had shimmered away, was gone.

Claire.

It was the last candle left within the Indian Agent. The last glimmer.

He curled himself around it to keep it alive, and when the storm inhaled he studied his right hand, could feel her beside him in the carriage that night and, as if he could insist on this, looked up the depression he was calling a road, for the cabman's blindered horse, huffing through the snow, its lanterns swinging. Claire waiting for him on the worn velvet seat.

He would get in a thousand times, just to have her hold her hand out to him.

And then never get out.

Only—

He ripped his eyes away.

Only—no. To ask for this, to ask that Claire come to retrieve him, to ferry him, it would be the same as asking the world to creak into a new shape, one in which she was dead as well, or dying, instead of living her full life, with whomever her father had ~~probably~~ *surely* chosen for her by now.

And it wouldn't be fair to ask her to give that up.

To join him here.

Better that she were happy, content, untroubled.

The Indian Agent held her name in his mouth now but shook his head no, that he wasn't going to say it.

Yet…he laughed, felt his eyes warm with heat he could no longer spare.

The cabman's horse. It was coming anyway.

The Indian Agent for the Blackfeet shook his head no, fell back into the snow and pushed off again, running as fast the other way as he could manage, falling time and again, the horse dogging him, tireless, just placing one large hoof after the other.

Around the next corner, no longer even certain he was in the depression anymore, the Indian Agent fell into another, a deeper rut, and took it, even though the crust in it was more brittle.

It was the track Yellow Tail's horse had left, dragging the Indian Agent's dead horse. Running from it.

The Indian Agent ran on all fours to keep the wind from pushing, and so he wouldn't lose the track.

At the end of it would be the saddlebags, and an extra blanket. An animal that knew the contours of the reservation, could possibly lead the Agent to shelter, to—

But then the rut stopped.

The Indian Agent fell over the stiff body of his dead horse. The braided rope had snapped in the cold.

The Indian Agent sat on his knees on top of his dead horse, patted it once though neither could feel it, then leaned forward, following now the ghosts of hoof prints, some of them already obliterated by the storm. The general direction, though. He could make it, had to.

As for the horse, it seemed to be following other, slighter depressions.

The Indian Agent wasn't the only one aware of the encampment of the dead, all around.

It made tracking Yellow Tail's horse both easier and worse. Easier because when the tracks had blown away, he still knew where the road was. Worse because, after two more winding turns the tracks became fresher, and then started stepping through other tracks. The Agent's own.

It hadn't been the cabman's horse trying to run him down, but Yellow Tail's.

The Indian Agent stood, looked behind him and then to the side. The green building was there in its transparent way, but Yellow Tail had slouched off.

Perhaps he'd seen his horse pass by and then come back to himself, remembered what he was supposed to be doing here. Perhaps he'd even mounted it at a run, as it passed, chasing the Agent.

The Agent looked behind him, deeper into the snow.

If the horse were following him, then it would be better to backtrack himself now than to keep running around the outhouse.

So he did, shuffling, stumbling, refusing to lie down each time he fell, until he found himself at a curve in the road he was unfamiliar with. A trackless stretch, where neither he nor the horse had been.

All around him still, the lights, the spirits of the dead, the starved.

The Agent stood there, and stood there, and finally screamed out to them that he was sorry, that he didn't know, that nobody could have known, that he only meant to…that he never intended to hurt anybody, that it hurt him too, that it was Collins, not him, that nobody could have—that, that…what did they *want*? To punish him? To see him suffer as they had?

And then he stopped screaming.

Surely that was it: *as they had.*

The only fitting sentence for his crimes would be to live as they did, as they had. As an Indian.

It was why the girl he'd kissed up against the wall had black hair instead of blonde, and those perfect, heavier-than-the-world fingertips.

It was why he'd been remembering another's life.

It was his punishment, to become Blackfeet, to be Piegan. To live on the reservation he'd created, the situation he was already leaving behind. To replace his own life with an Indian one, and thus know firsthand the end result of his policies. An end result generations away from last Winter, just so he could see the scope of what he'd done, that it still had traceable effect. So that, in a sense, he could be inflicting it upon himself.

He nodded, accepted this.

It was the only explanation.

And Yellow Tail had sensed this somehow.

Would he go to Lead Feather now, though?

The Agent looked around at this…this *town.*

It was ridiculous.

Would his new life, his sentence, would it start when he finally succumbed to the cold, or would it happen by degrees, so that what he was forgetting of himself would feel as though nothing, go unmissed, so stealthy would the replacement be.

For longer than he dared if he hoped to move again, the Indian Agent stood in the wind. Just staring. But then a shimmer to his right pulled his head around.

It wasn't one of the dead as he expected, but a hole in the storm. A *lodge* hole.

The Agent cocked his head over, disbelieving.

The flap on the lodge had become unfastened, blown over so that, for a few ragged, flapping moments, the fire within was a pale glow.

And then a dark hand reached out, pulled the flap shut.

It was the hand of a boy.

The Indian Agent could feel his heart in his chest.

No, said aloud. *No.*

It couldn't be, not him, he couldn't be here.

If he was…if he was, then that meant—

But it couldn't be. The Agent wouldn't allow it.

That hand, that arm, that boy.

He was supposed to be in the corner of Catches Weasel's dugout. *Alive.*

Stone.

The lodge was stone.

The Indian Agent didn't understand.

The Piegan followed the buffalo. Their dwellings were moveable. And even if they weren't, they had no mortar, possessed no means of fashioning stone into the shape of one of their lodges. The closest they ever came to permanence were holes dug into soft banks that, even when braced with wood, still tended to collapse if abandoned for too long.

But perhaps in this encampment of the dead, they had—perhaps there was no longer any reason to make a lodge such that it could be dragged behind a horse. Even here, there were no buffalo to follow, and so, over the years, the lodges had become more solid dwellings, only retaining their former shape because the Piegan were most comfortable in interior spaces that were narrower at the top, circular around where they sat, and slept.

The Agent lifted the flap and held it for a moment, allowing the boy within to see him—even in the storm, it was custom—and then he fell through, was insensible for he knew not how long.

When he could see again he was under two robes, and his clothes had melted, and the fire should have been warm but wasn't.

And the boy, he was watching the Indian Agent.

Not Lead Feather.

The Indian Agent slept again, woke to a lower fire, one that had heat now.

The boy still sitting there. His hair long like Claire would have expected, his chest sunken. He was fifteen, maybe. Just staring.

I'm dead, the Indian Agent said, finally.

The boy nodded, said in English that he was too, yeah. It happens.

Yellow Tail, the Agent said then, in explanation for his presence there, but this only caused the boy to narrow his eyes, study the Agent from another angle.

What? the Indian Agent asked.

Nobody calls him that.

The Agent couldn't think of a fitting response to this, so let his eyes roam over the inside of the lodge. It was stone here too, rough like a cat's tongue, and painted in layers, by many hands over many years.

All around, instead of bowls and robes, were muddy brown bottles and brittle waxy paper.

And you stay here now? the Agent said to the boy, his voice almost a whisper.

The boy nodded as if this was a child's question, beneath answering. His face slack with disinterest, his eyes ready to flick away, to the words painted onto the wall, the pictures and numbers and burn marks.

My horse, the Agent said.

The boy just stared.

I don't—the Agent started, then couldn't finish. Do you have a name?

The boy shrugged, hugged his knees, looked to the lodge walls again.

Where does the smoke go, you think? he said.

The Agent looked up, to the top of the lodge, and the boy was right: there was no hole smudged black by years of smoke.

The Agent didn't answer, held his hand out to the fire instead. It was warm. He closed his eyes, and while they were closed the boy said *Jamie*.

Jamie?

The boy nodded.

Not Runs Inside or Yellow Kidney or Sees Otter or Sleeps Twice—or Heavy Lodge? the Agent said, holding his arms out to the stone walls.

Just Jamie. It not Indian enough for you?

I'm—I'm...

The Indian Agent couldn't recall his own name, though. Just *Sam*.

His lip trembled. The shift was already occurring.

Claire, he said to himself, in resistance.

The boy laughed.

We've both got girl names then, yeah? he said.

He was holding one of the brown bottles across to the Agent, just as Yellow Tail had.

This time the Agent took it, looked in it.

It was empty, caked with dirt.

We don't need the other kind anymore, the boy said, smiling, and the Agent looked to the hole he'd fallen through.

In a stone lodge, the outside world, the storm, the cold, none of it existed. Just this. Forever.

I think I froze to death, the Agent said aloud.

The boy scrounged another bottle from the dirt and nodded, said him too.

What?

Freon, paleface.

The Agent let his eyes unfocus over all this.

I don't know what freon is, the Agent said. Am I supposed to?

It's not bad, I guess. Well, I mean, except that you die sometimes.

This was funny to him, made him look away to smile, embarrassed to be the only one getting the joke.

He drank again. Drank nothing. The memory of the alcohol or opiate the bottle had once held.

The Indian Agent watched him, didn't look away.

You said nobody calls him that.

What?

Yellow Tail.

The boy wasn't smiling now.

We're not supposed to talk about them, he said.

Who?

Them. You know. Out there with the real beer.

Then who can we talk about?

Why do you even want to talk at all?

Because—because I don't know this place.

Browning, you mean?

The Agent felt his throat swell.

It was real then.

He nodded.

Shit, the boy said, tipping the bottle up as if to study its contents, its dust and air, that's all you want to know about?

Browning, the Agent repeated, like a devotional term.

It made the boy smile, shake his head in disbelief.

It's easy, he said, shrugging. Say

a boy is born in the back room of a house on the street everybody calls Death Row. In the front room, a football game's blasting. The boy's dad isn't watching that game. As far as anybody knows, he's out around Seattle somewhere, or Portland, maybe Tacoma. But the boy's mom gives the boy his dad's name anyway, just so if he doesn't ever sign the papers making it legal, that the boy's his and he has to pay, then that name will always remind the dad of what he should have done.

So already the boy's a poker chip, out there in the middle of the table between everybody. Not that the mom doesn't hold him close, or finally make her big sister go into the living room to turn the game down.

Two minutes later, one green bar at a time, the volume's back up where it was, maybe even a click or two louder. But it was important for the mom to at least make that gesture, and important to let the sister who still had four months to go think she was doing something, that she was fighting too, protecting this baby, this boy. Because he's special, this one. Isn't going to be like the rest.

To prove it, the mom decides she isn't even going to ever have any other kids, just because she wants to be able to focus all of herself on this one.

It's a lie of course, but holding her son, it doesn't feel like a lie.

As to why that street's called Death Row, it's the government program: you can only get a house there if you're an elder. So what happens is all the old people put their name on the list, and if they get a house, all their children move in with them, and the children's children, until Indians are stacked on Indians, spilling out all the windows and doors, sometimes just exploding out into the night, half of them not ever coming back.

And that's how it's always been, even since the bow and arrow days.

Three years later the boy's dad is back on the reservation. Just a rumor at first, somebody whispering the dad's name to the mom like a question almost, like it's not their fault he came back, but then a gold Buick with mismatched fenders is easing by the house after the lights are off.

As for the papers the boy's dad's supposed to have signed, he hasn't seen them yet. Hasn't seen the boy's mom for nearly four years now.

What he's doing driving by is seeing if there's a truck that's always there, that doesn't belong. A new him.

There isn't.

There had been until two years ago, but then one day when that boyfriend was supposed to be watching the boy for the six hours of the mom's shift, he thought it would be all right to leave the boy with one of his ex-girlfriends.

The mom came home to no son, no note, no nothing, finally found her boyfriend shooting bottles north of town, on the road across to Whiskey Gap. Him and his friend had run out of bottles twice already, had to go back for more cases. Like that's the only reason they were drinking, to have something to sight in on.

When the boyfriend set his rifle down to shape an excuse in the air with his hands, the boy's mom took it, held it at her hip and took a step back, to get the barrel out of his reach.

The boyfriend stopped talking.

She had the sling wrapped around her front hand like she knew how to shoot, maybe.

Had he already had it cocked when he heard her car crunching up behind him, though? Was the safety on?

It wasn't just a gesture this time. The boy's mom was crying in every way but with her eyes, and the story of it finally made it back to the boy's dad two years later when he came back.

He was working a crew with a bunch of guys who'd been in ninth grade when he was supposed to have been a senior. The boyfriend was one of their big brothers, from the basketball team that had made it all the way to Butte, so the way the dad heard the story was that she was crazy, this mom.

The crew telling him this was too young to remember that the mom was his ex, though. Or, not even his ex, really. The way he looked at it, it was more like he'd just had to leave for a while.

But now he was back.

What they were doing that day was stacking cinderblock into a fence.

The dad kept stacking until the truck came for them.

In the old days, the boy's mom would have gotten a name for what she did: Shoots the Car Twice or Four Holes in the Glass or Doesn't Ever Learn or Can't Stop Fighting.

Now, though, everybody just calls her by her usual name. But some of the kids still hold imaginary rifles up when she's around. Growing up, the boy won't understand this, will think at first, without telling anybody, or asking, that his mom is marked in some tribal way and that everybody knows it. That that's why they all hold rifles when she's around. But then, for a secret couple of weeks before his uncle tells him the story, shows him that boyfriend, how he is now, the boy will allow himself to think that his mom's a chief of some kind, if the Blackfeet even let women do that. But they probably would, for her.

It's just a stupid story, though. His mom, jacking another shell home, the butt of the stock against her thigh, the barrel making these small circles in the air, the boyfriend shuffling from side to side, trying not to be in any of those circles, having no idea that the reason he's almost getting shot here is that the ex he'd left the boy with had had to go around the mountain to Kalispell for some reason, and had known better than to leave the boy in her house, as he'd be proof for her current boyfriend that she was still talking to *her* old boyfriend. So the boy had been missing for the whole afternoon, presumed stolen or lost or worse. By the time he showed back up, got passed to grandparents and aunts to deliver to the mom on Death Row, the tribal police had already been there to talk to the mom about the four rounds she'd, according to her now-ex, accidentally shot into his car.

She hadn't talked to them, though.

Instead of answering the door, she'd stayed locked in the bathroom. What she was doing was carving her son's initials into her left forearm with the jagged tip of a broken beer bottle.

It was a deal she was making, an apology to the boy, not a suicide attempt, but they took her away that night anyway, for observation, and when both officers weren't enough to pry her arms from around her boy, they called in the retired game warden too—he was already next door—and finally packed her into the car, then the observation room, to wait for the doctor to make rounds. It took long enough that she opened her bandages, bled into the sheets. And maybe she really was trying to kill herself then. Just because everything was so stupid. Because nobody would let her be with her boy—a story the boy heard one time when she was in jail again. This time it was his aunt telling it to him. As an apology. Maybe an explanation. Because after that first time, it was like the mom was on a string, one that was tied to the front door of the jail.

But it was all because she loved him so much, the aunt said to the boy, holding him by the shoulders so he could understand.

He was eight by then, not saying all that much. Just watching everything.

The first fight he got in was because of his dad. Because a kid at school made some joke about the boy's dad, his name, then wouldn't take it back.

He lost that first time, and the second, but by sixth grade he'd learned that the only real trick was not to care if they hurt you. To just keep hitting and kicking anyway.

And his uncles, they'd sit in the living room and smile like they remembered all those fights themselves. That they're what make you tough, get you ready.

By then the boy was watching football with them, even getting the last drink from a beer every now and again, if his mom wasn't there. Sometimes if she was.

It was one of the times when he went to the Town Pump with his ex-uncle who still lived with them that he saw his mom's old boyfriend, the one she just laughed about now, like she hadn't really been going to shoot him anyway.

He was ghosting around the pumps, like he was waiting for somebody.

The boy's head rotated, watching the boyfriend as his uncle eased past.

The boy's right eye was still tinged green, from two weeks ago when he'd pulled in-school suspension.

He could feel it, was proud of it in a dull way.

But then his uncle jerked the truck into park before it was all the way stopped.

The boy planted his hand on the dash, looked over.

The uncle hooked his head back to the pumps, asked the boy if he knew who that was, yeah?

The boy shook his head no, then got the part of the story his aunt hadn't told him: the Town Pump Indian had been the shooter for that team that was supposed to have gone to state back when. They'd been the Indians like every other

Blackfeet team, but because they were all the sons of guilty parents, they'd been brought up traditional, with the sweats on Sundays and the grass dance competitions and drums and all that, so what they called themselves was the Longhairs. The photographers loved them, put them all over the papers. But they were good too, weren't just the only team that got their hair braided before every game. And the Town Pump Indian, he was their shooter. All he knew was the bottom of the net.

Sitting behind the wheel of his stopped truck, the boy's uncle leaned back as if holding the ball, waiting for the defender to finally drift back down to earth.

It was magic, or close enough.

What then? the boy asked.

The uncle shrugged, chocked his door open, said Then nothing. Down in Butte they lost to a team they'd beat twice already, once in district, once before that.

It wasn't enough, though.

The boy waited for the rest.

His uncle smiled, watching somebody through the window of the store.

Don't tell your mom I told you this, he said, locking eyes with the boy so the boy would understand, and then he told the backside of the story the boy thought he knew, about the time he'd gone to Kalispell for the afternoon: it was his dad, back in town two or three years after the rifle and the windshield and the mom in observation, bleeding into the sheets. Because the dad was still dragging a couple of bench warrants, he was playing quiet, but he was there, and heard what had happened.

The boy stared at the dash and tried to see it all in his head.

By then his main memories of his dad mostly had to do with the front yard, and people screaming, and the sound of gravel hitting the side of the house, and deer left gutted on the porch for his grandparents to cut into stew. This from his uncle was the first he was really hearing of his dad, at least without his mom there to flare her eyes out at whoever was talking.

See his face? the boy's uncle asked, about the Town Pump Indian, the last of the Longhairs.

The boy nodded, had. It was pitted and scarred, and, on one side, caved in some.

He was in a wreck, the boy said. Right?

You could say that, the uncle said back, hiding most of his smile with his hand. Or you could say that your old man dropped by to see him. From about fifty feet straight *up*.

This was funny enough to the uncle that he stepped down from the truck, slammed the door behind him, went to talk to whoever he'd seen in the store.

In the cab, the boy looked up from the dash, at the Town Pump Indian, working his way around the backside of the far pumps now.

The way he was broken meant that the boy's dad loved him, the boy. That he'd been mad the kid had gone to Kalispell that day. That he was protecting the boy, just after the fact, as best he could, the only way he knew.

The boy held onto this with both eyes.

By eighth grade he'd learned how to burn shapes and initials into the back of his hands with pencil erasers. When his mom saw it she hit him. It was the only time. To make up for it she bought him a movie, let him stay up late watching it. The next day he rubbed ink into his burn anyway. It was a foggy arrowhead, or supposed to be.

His mom pretended it wasn't there.

His dad was living with them by then. Now the deer he brought home, he hung up by their back legs from a metal swingset frame beside the house. The boy's job was to keep the dogs off it until his mom could cut it up, which she always had to do before morning, or else the game warden would see it didn't have a tag, and was a muley doe anyway, in April or some other illegal month.

At first the boy used a water hose to keep the dogs away, but then the dogs quit caring so he had to use a board, then a piece of rebar. Finally what worked best was an antenna he twisted off his dad's gold Buick that was up on blocks. He thought the antenna worked because the dogs didn't understand it—it was skinny enough and fast enough that they couldn't see it, could only feel it, then have no explanation for the sting in their skin.

In between dogs, the boy would talk to the deer, apologize to it but say how they were going to eat it, so it was all right. And then he would cup the deer's jaw in his hand as if giving it something, or listening. He never was sure, really. But it felt right.

What his dad always said was he was going to start taking the boy out with him soon. To learn to be a real Indian.

To Tacoma, you mean? the mom would ask. Or Portland?

Hunting, the boy's dad would say, his lips thin like hers.

It was like a joke, just one nobody ever laughed at.

The next time the boy saw the Longhair shooter up close was at a basketball game. The boy was in tenth grade by then, had never learned to play. He was good at smuggling beers into the stands, though.

What the Longhair shooter was doing, aside from not getting close to anybody, like he knew they wouldn't want him to, was watching the game. Watching a specific player, the boy was pretty sure. The star. He had the long hair too, and didn't drink or go out all weekend or anything. Already his scholarship letters were piling up.

At halftime, the boy and his cousin went to the parking lot and kicked in the car door of a guy who'd taken their money for beer last weekend, then not come back. It was nothing new. Or, the only thing new was that, from under the stands, the boy was pretty sure the Longhair was watching him.

For a few breaths, the boy stopped kicking the door, just stared back, lost, but then the window glass shattered too loud and they had to run.

The team lost that night, and most of that season, but it was because their star was only a sophomore then.

The next year was going to be their year, the year the whole town would shut down to make a game, the year everybody knew all the stats, all the other teams, everything.

The boy was sixteen that year, driving when he had a car, or at least some keys, and of all the funerals he'd been to so far, the only one that he still thought about was his friend's, that first night they'd all tried some new stuff, and then tried to keep the friend alive with more of the new stuff, and more, and then almost had to face charges for it, and then been jumped twice so far by the dead friend's older cousins for it, beatings the boy took though he didn't have to.

What the boy thought about on accident the most, he supposed, were the deer. Not the ones he had to guard, and
learned to talk to finally, but the ones from before that, left
on the porch.

Instead of cutting right into them, his grandparents
would usually rouse the boy from bed, pull him bleary-eyed
to the front door, out into the cold in his underwear.

The deer would just be there, like from another world.
Their eyes open, tongues hanging, dry. Feet so perfect and
black, bellies slit open, hollowed out.

That was when the boy had started cupping their jaws in
his hands. Like that was the closest, most important part of
them. Or, second most important. The most important was
the picture they put in his head of his dad. Not in Seattle or
Tacoma or Portland, serving thirty days or hiding in a train
car or sitting at a table alone, ketchup packets arranged between his hands like pieces to a puzzle, but out there in the
old days, running deer down, stealing them from the wardens and slinging them across his shoulders, carrying them
into town to feed his family. Because that's what you have to
do.

The boy was pretty sure that was the lesson his grandparents wanted him to learn from the deer. That this is what
you do, provide. That meat can be an apology. That it can
be everything.

In the concrete tipi with his friend that night, even, the
white foam dribbling from his friend's mouth, his eyes rolled
back from the cold, his legs locked and shaking fast, he'd
even tried it on him instead of running away: cupped his jaw

in his palm, held it still, told him it was going to be all right, it was going to be okay.

It was a lie, but still, in that moment anyway, that rush of heat and motion in the jawbone as his friend's teeth ground to dust, it felt more real than anything.

The November after that, before the year that was going to be the basketball team's year, the boy cut his left wrist open. On accident, but, because he was his mom's son, nobody believed him. It wasn't suicide, though. It had been halftime of a football game, Thanksgiving, and he'd been outside watching his uncle adjust the timing on his Pontiac, and there was a sheetrock knife on top of an old battery, between the two terminals.

At first the boy only reached over to nudge it, to be sure it couldn't touch both posts at once and blow up, but then he had it in his hands, was rolling it across his fingers, and then, when his uncle looked up from under the hood, the boy said watch this, and sliced it down through the air at his left wrist.

What he didn't know was that the very top of the blade was still out. Just the tip, a rusty eighth of an inch.

It was enough.

His uncle slammed the hood and made the boy hold his arm out the window the whole two blocks to the hospital, to make the blood cooler, thicker, slower, and when the uncle twisted the ignition back in the emergency lane the timing was jacked up enough that the engine wouldn't even die, so the uncle just got out anyway, carrying the boy, his youngest sister's first son. Behind him his Pontiac, still in gear, plowed gently into three other cars, so that, instead of being a hero, he got arrested for no insurance, and negligence, and whatever else he already had behind him.

The boy was home that time by the end of the game, his mom watching him with her cry eyes. She wasn't mad at him yet about getting his uncle in jail, and was still pretending he didn't have that blurry blue triangle on the back of his hand.

That night after everybody was asleep he went out the front door and all the way across town to the concrete tipi his friend had died in, and slept there without a jacket, like that could make up for anything, and then wrote on the inside wall that the police sucked.

It was the only thing he could think of.

Later that summer, in the hospital for a week and half, mostly observation, the nurse who walked into his room to change his drip or turn the blinds or whatever she had to do at the front of her shift, she stopped a few steps in, would only look at him in pieces.

He didn't know what to do.

There was the vague idea that her daughter was a couple of grades below him, maybe, before he'd quit, but he was pretty sure that daughter was under strict orders not to talk to him too. Because he was already getting to be one of the bad Indians.

That wasn't it, though.

The nurse covered her mouth with her hand and ran out of the room.

The boy's IV dripped to a stop.

An hour later she was back, standing by his bed when he opened his eyes. Her hand was cupping his jaw. He let his hand cover hers, keep it there.

You don't remember me, she said.

He shook his head no, he didn't.

She smiled, swallowed, looked away, to sixteen years ago.

I took you to Kalispell once, she said, her eyes wet now.

He stared down into his sheets, nodded.

Your mom still hates me for it, she added.

He just stared.

I didn't—I didn't understand then, the nurse said, almost like a question. It wasn't like I was going to lose you or anything, right?

Now the boy looked up to her.

She shook her head at herself.

But. God. When I had mine...I don't know. I understood, understand. I would have killed me too. Really.

The boy nodded.

What did— he started. What did we...you do?

In Kalispell?

Yes.

The nurse had to turn her head to the side to remember, to be sure. But then it was funny to her. She laughed through her nose a bit.

My brother, she said. He was dating this girl from Babb, I don't know. She had these eyes, everybody was in love with her that year—but, yeah. He came back from her place once with this smelly old bundle, and hid it in my room. He owed me money though, for what he'd done with my hair curler. So when he left at lunch that day, I took that pack, that bundle thing—it smelled like mothballs, probably wasn't even old—and sold it in Kalispell. Forty dollars, yeah? I got a curler and a dryer and everything.

The boy smiled with one side of his mouth.

We used to sell all that stuff back then, the nurse said. It was in every closet, yeah? Oh, and some people wanted to take a picture with you too. That's right.

He looked to her.

A white couple, she said. I had to say yes. They thought you were mine, I mean. It was all like a joke. Until we got back, I mean.

Now the boy laughed through his nose, tried to keep his smile real.

The nurse stood, adjusted his IV though it probably didn't need it, then patted the mattress beside his arm, then left.

The boy stared at the empty door.

Two days later, the first of the month, he woke with two crisp twenties folded into his hand.

What he really wanted was the picture.

The reason he was in the hospital this time was that he'd put a plastic shopping bag over his head and then worked a rubber band down after it, so it was tight around his neck, and then superglued his hands to the steering wheel so he couldn't change his mind, and then dry-swallowed all the pills already melting in his mouth.

Where he did it was in the front seat of his mom's car. She didn't know he'd taken it. It was three in the morning, in the parking lot of the hospital. He sat behind the wheel with the engine ticking down for a full hour before finally nodding, emptying the bottle into his mouth and reaching over to the passenger seat for the bag, the rubber band already doubled over the last three fingers of his right hand, a nail ready to punch through the side of the superglue tube so he could rub it into his skin like lotion.

The doctors wrote it up as his second suicide attempt in six months—five, really—and they weren't all the way wrong. But they weren't all the way right either.

It was complicated.

If the boy had left a note, it would have had a lot to do with the Longhair watching him from under the bleachers with his crushed-in face. Always watching him from under the bleachers.

But it would have had to do with that time he went to Kalispell, too.

And with his uncle who had to go to jail for him that time.

And his friend who died in the concrete tipi.

All the typical, easy stuff, yeah, but the other stuff too, that shouldn't hurt: the time in the fourth grade he gave his chocolate milk to the girl he'd secretly decided to someday marry; the letter his dad had written from Oregon that time, that the boy's mom hadn't even opened but just left on the table for the boy to decide, like he was old enough now; the time he'd had the perfect amount of beer and smoke in him at a basketball game, so that when the Longhair's son, or whoever he was to him, when he pivoted on the baseline away from the defender and then rose up, hung and finally released, falling down out of bounds like that had been his only purpose in life, to make that shot, the boy had flown up from his chair with everybody else, screaming like everything was going to be all right now. That he'd saved them all. That no other moment mattered but this one.

Except then, after that game and all the rest, after the season was over too early, everybody already waiting for next year, that star player missed one practice, then two, then didn't even make the Sunday pick-up game to play half-speed and still show up all the has-beens.

When the coach went to check on him, he was curled around himself in bed, staring at the wall. In the toilet down the hall, unflushed, yellowy thin blood.

The boy was deep into the night when he heard, and it was funny, it was fair, it was the reservation finally catching up with that star player the same way it had always been catching up with everybody else. Now the star was just going to be down at the usual level, or maybe even lower, because he knew what it was like to have made a perfect shot.

Soon, when the star could walk again, the boy knew, when his star kidneys kicked back in enough with weekly dialysis, he'd be in an old fatigue jacket, slouching around the Town Pump too, mumbling to himself, holding his fingers before his face just to watch them move, like they used to be all different.

For some reason this made the boy drink harder, and hold it in longer, and even once, like it could balance somehow, he went with his cousin to one of his cousin's ex-girlfriend's and played sloppy drunk basketball until they each threw up into the tall grass and couldn't stop laughing.

But then one morning he couldn't get out of bed, and then when he could, he didn't.

His cousin came over to drag him here or there but he just rolled tighter into the sheets, stared at the wall.

What if that white family in Kalispell had just taken him, back then?

He hated himself for even thinking it, but thought it all the same, on accident.

With his thumbnail he was carving another line beside the scar on his left wrist. Under the sheets where he didn't have to see.

Four days later his cousin brought him a beer still cold from the cooler but the boy shook his head no, then got into a fight with his cousin in the living room and knocked over all the furniture and most of the pictures, but he didn't end up laughing like usual. Just bleeding, and staring at his cousin as his cousin walked away, into town and whatever the night had to offer, or take back.

The boy's grandfather started to ask him something but the boy held his hands up like he was under attack, or like he already knew, retreated back to his room. The next time he came out, for a handful of the cereal he'd just thought of, his uncle was on the couch, flipping through the satellite channels. The boy stood in the doorway and watched the shows then finally sat on the couch too, not saying anything, him and his uncle just watching like they were studying for some test they knew was coming.

Three days later, two days before the last day everybody knew the star player could get surgery and start recuperating, be ready for next season, the boy found the plastic grocery bag. At first it was just a crinkling noise for his fingers under the front edge of the couch, but then, once he studied it, it became an answer. The only answer.

Two days from then he has his mom's keys, her car, is in the parking lot working the safety cap on the brown bottle.

The plan is to die, so, technically, it is suicide, but it's not any of the usual Indian ways. He's not getting shot or driving off a cliff or freezing in the snow or drowning in vomit or getting beat up by too many people at once or catching leukemia or trains or knives or any of that. Just because all those would probably mess his body up too much. Not leave enough.

That's why he has the headlights on. So he can get found before too many minutes have passed.

Through the blue plastic of the bag, the hospital is a cartoon.

He smiles, breathes in, the thin plastic following his breath into his mouth, his palms and undersides of his fingers hot with glue, already fixed in place, the pills powdery and bitter in the back of his throat, where he's trying not to throw up, because he's suddenly more afraid of drowning than of suffocating.

It's how he's seeing himself that's important, though.

How he's seeing himself is the way he used to see his dad, reflected in the shiny eyes of the deer left on the porch: as somebody good, somebody doing the only good thing they can. Providing meat.

Only it isn't the nurses or visitors who finally find him.

They're all busy with the three other high schoolers who've tried donating organs that night. Two of them have done it like the boy, on purpose, for the sake of the team, the town, the tribe, and the other one's just done it the usual way: his car rolling end over end through the grass.

Though one of the organ donors will die, still, it's the car-wreck Indian's kidneys that end up working best. He's the star player's old nephew, just turned eighteen last week. And maybe his wreck *was* on purpose, too. That's what everybody starts saying, anyway, almost as soon as they hear.

But the boy doesn't know any of this then.

All he's doing is dying, exactly three hundred feet from

the room he was born in, and then he's dead, so never feels the glass shattering in over him.

It's his cousin, who saw *his* cousin's mom's car in the parking lot of the hospital. Where it shouldn't have been.

He lifts the boy from the front seat, his head hanging limp backwards, the skin of his fingers tearing away from the steering wheel.

Because the cousin's hands are full, he reaches down with his teeth, tears the plastic bag away from the boy's mouth, who he isn't going to let die too, because if he dies, then there'll be only him, the cousin, left. And he should have been dead himself three years ago already, lost in the snow, part of the mountain, the Park, just another tourist attraction, another stupid statistic.

So he spits the plastic out, screams at the boy, who still isn't waking up or even coughing, even moving, and then he just screams straight up at the reservation, promising that if the boy can only *live*, live like he's supposed to, like he *has* to, then he'll do anything, whatever. That it's so so idiotic that he can't even save *one* Indian, that that's all he's asking for here, just the chance to save one, please, just to not let one more die, not tonight, not like this.

And, because he asks hard enough, loud enough, a nurse just coming back on shift hears, and breathes life into his cousin, the boy who doesn't want it, then doesn't believe it, but by that time the cousin's gone into the night again, and all the other nights too, only stopping long enough to eat sometimes, or sleep, or, once for four weeks in a row, go to some of his junior year of high school, write a couple of papers, one for his friend, who died, and one for his cousin, who lived. But he gets an F on the one about the Indian who lived. Because it's obviously copied from some history book in his house. He hasn't even bothered to change any of the names, the teacher says, or make it sound like an essay, or like himself at all. Instead it's just a series of old time letters, each of them starting with

Claire—

Yellow Tail forces my hand to this page. Not my heart, that goes to you any way, but this last series of missives to you. When I argued with him that I had not enough paper to detail what he wanted and how, he produced a leather bound sheaf from Catches Weasel's kindling stores. I write now on the backside of the pages he's torn out, and in the French he claims to be able to read but refuses to read aloud.

Know also that if you're reading this, then I am passed.

Know also that you can not trust it, unless it is in my own hand, and if antique English with ornamental lettering is bleeding up through the paper to mix with my ink. If what you read now is typed, however, then understand the means by which it came to be that way—Yellow Tail, standing in the doorway of the Agency office some time in the Spring, angling my hand written pages over to better catch the afternoon light, so he can sound the French aloud to Doreen, sitting faithfully at the Caligraph your father burdened me with on parting, perhaps to ease my correspondence or to better impersonalize it, or because he thought I spoke always without thinking, and thus needed the slowness of key entry to deliberate upon my words, Doreen of course in the possession of no French, only the Piegan and English her post requires, meaning that Yellow Tail has to take the French of my uneven hand writing in and speak it out in Piegan, for

Doreen to record in English on a machine she has no familiarity with. But even that is not the final concern. The final concern is that Yellow Tail will in all likelihood be smiling his distinctive smile as he angles those hand written sheets over, smiling where Doreen can not see, or else she would know he is inserting his own fabrications and omitting certain other details that do not suit his intent, that do not suit my defamation.

Not that such defamation is not inevitable.

I make no claims of innocence, Claire. Unless that can be a measure of the purity of one's intentions.

But even then.

And perhaps it is this very reluctance that alerted Yellow Tail not to the nature of my crimes, those are manifest, but to the nature of my punishment, which is this letter he insists I pen.

Yet when I resist his proposition of writing these pages, he never fails to remind me in his apologetic way that did he not finally find me in the snow, and then go after me even when I ran into the storm, and then go after me a second time even?

But of course I ameliorate.

Finally, I do not write this out of a sense of indebtedness, nor because it was his geographical agility that led us to this mound like all the rest, under which was this impossible dugout, but—

You'll remember of course that the Deputy Commissioner warned me about dealings with Indians.

However, I am not the same Agent I was fourteen months ago.

Are you in fact reading this, Yellow Tail? If so, then you have already discovered that I have not yet begun to write what you have asked me to write, and yet I am mere minutes from handing this brittle page across the fire to you and then nodding with defeated solemnity as if the story is duly begun.

If you study it as you do with your eyes both savage and cunning and then fold it into the oil cloth in your pack, satisfied, then, Claire, I'm talking to you now, through whomever Yellow Tail has trusted to read my French aloud to Doreen.

I will relate more after tonight, after this. About Yellow Tail's visions, which hold me hostage and force my hand, and about…about other things, which I can not yet trust here, and perhaps can not trust at all.

And, Yellow Tail, if you have in fact struggled this far through my sloping hand, then know that you have talked in your sleep as well, friend, and longingly.

Not in Piegan, but in French.

Your wife's name, I believe, that your superstitions forbid you to say. The Maleury I've been mistaking for a curse, when in fact it was communion. As you know, it is a word that means poor luck, that means disfortunate.

Again, condolences.

And know that I'm watching your face as you study this.

Francis Dalimpere

Claire—

I have decided that there is no way I can encode this such that Yellow Tail can not alter its meaning. Take the initial missive if you will, already torn from this cached journal. It begins with the words Yellow Tail forces my hand.

What if he leaves that intact as ruse, then changes or replaces a subsequent correspondence? Is his sense of deceit that sophisticated? And how far back into this correspondence might his sense of justice take him?

Or what if he anticipated my cumbersome deceit, and has allowed for it? What if my written French slips past him as I want, now, tonight, but then he catches it in the eventual Spring when standing between Doreen and whoever he has found that can read for her?

Perhaps the only mark of authenticity possible is not my hand at all, for if these sheets are typed then there is no manner in which I could have signed them in the way you must be familiar with, if any of my posts have reached you at all.

But still, always, there is room for error, for words not my own to be in my mouth, as memories not my own already pollute my nights. And more.

Already, without any prompting, my hand trembles to write what Yellow Tail wants me to write, using you as my confessor, as if your forgiveness or understanding can cleanse me.

And it is so cold.

And as in my recurrent dream, the one that was of the unhappened future but that now is of the experienced past, I have had no recourse but to fix Yellow Tail's back in my sight, and plod on.

But I have not yet dreamed the next part, when we arrived at this dugout.

The only portion I know with any surety is that this letter and no other will I fold into my own clothes, close to my skin.

If it finds you some how, then know not only that you are a widow, but that I was plundered as well.

I love you.

I love you.

I say it in English as well because it does not sound the same in French.

Fr.

Claire—

It is still the same night. I know not if it is by accident or a product of cleverness that Yellow Tail has left this antique journal with me. And perhaps it doesn't matter. He is gone, as is Catches Weasel and Catches Weasel's wife, whose name she refuses to allow me. I am horseless, with only enough wood to last the night, the boy dying across the fire from me in spite of my prayers, and the deals I long to make, or have already made.

Perhaps where Yellow Tail and Catches Weasel have gone is to some secret grove of lodge pole pines, from which they mean to fashion a scaffold for the boy.

Or perhaps their intention is that I be forced to watch him die, and be unable to render assistance, unable even to speak his language in order to comfort him, able instead only to run my fingers over his hair, which already wants to enwrap my fingers, pull me back to last Winter.

But I swallow it down again and again.

And I have not yet told you Yellow Tail's vision, I know. Or the vision he claims with a smile, as he only has to suggest that he saw it in his sleep and I flesh out the rest, from my own fears and guilt.

Claire.

Your name is what I have left. For however long I now have before the storm draws me to its bosom, which will be my final resting place.

And now I am back from standing in the black coldness outside the lodge, on the foundationless surety that Yellow Tail would be out there, his silent exit due either to some intricacy of the weather only the Piegan are aware of or to some migration of game the Piegan have been tuned into for generation upon generation.

But standing outside the lodge, I was alone. For miles.

I dared not even say your name, for it would slip away on the wind.

We are five days hard travel from Badger Creek, north and east, and by my reckoning have only crossed what usually takes one half of one day.

May chance I would leave me to my own devices as well. As payment. For Maleury, and the rest.

Is this a test Yellow Tail has arranged, not so different from the test I was giving him in French in my prior missive?

Will he only come back once I have written what he asked?

But how would he know?

Perhaps I am yet dead, and only do not know it. Perhaps this is a thing Yellow Tail could discern, watching me sleep. Or perhaps we in fact are those two dead trappers, talking now to each other in French, trying only to remember each other so we can find the way to our common home.

Yet still I reach out across these frozen plains for you, Claire. Always. And it grips me that if I stop writing on the backs of these sheets, or if my inkwell runs dry, then my connection to you, my relation, it will have drawn to a close.

And so I impress the pen less deeply now, as a feather touches dust without disturbing it, as lightly as a mother's breath as she leans down to whisper the future to her dearly sleeping child.

If you can read this now, it means the light in Spring was particularly intense. Or perhaps pure is the more accurate term, though I can see that quality of sun even now, and how the dust is alight in it, as a thing alive.

And I only want to say your name a thousand times, to string it across the distance between us.

But to cry in words is perhaps natural at moments such as these, and would help neither of us.

Instead of that, allow me to proffer what Yellow Tail claims was his vision the night past, which he told me upon seeing the cavalry cattle bunched against the wind yesterday, as if they were the trigger that fired his memory. In the vision, which he relates unquestioned, as gospel, my horse that broke free from the Agency stalls in advance of the storm has nearly killed itself running to the pens it knows the best, which are Sheffield's down to the west of Old Agency, below the newly removed Boundary. And there Yellow Tail, of course, ends his vision. But there I pick it up, Claire. If Sheffield goes outside to tap his pipe against his boot heel as is his custom after a full dinner and sees my horse standing there with no saddle, no reins, what is he to think? The party will be formed before dawn, and he will ride north with the stated purpose of ascertaining whether I've fallen victim to an Indian uprising, but in truth he knows the Piegan have other concerns right now, and is only bringing a party so that he can have witnesses to how I've mishandled my post and endangered the federal government's relations with a down-trod and fightless people.

So now, if I some how weather the storm and make my way back to Badger Creek, then it will only be to face

Sheffield's mockery, and the charges he's held back all year, to let grow in rumor more dire. And no, Claire, none of this is meant to suggest that by having gained Catches Weasel's dugout I can now some how avert or belay or other wise escape those charges.

Rather, and this serves to transform your father's suspicions of me into certainties, I have invested myself completely in the survival of one Indian boy, this Lead Feather whom I've already mentioned, in prior letters you will also never have received. My sincerest hope and most ill advised but heart felt gamble is that if I can just reach across the fire and force him to live, then these accidents of circumstance of which Yellow Tail now makes me write will be washed away, and the charges with them, both in this life and the next. Then it will be as if I never stayed on that boarding platform in St. Louis, but as if I instead were on the train with you, riding east, the sides of our hands touching so that we need not say anything at all.

But to get there I first have to tell you about last Winter, about Lincoln's holiday of Thanks Giving, as Yellow Tail requests. As to why this should be addressed to you and not to some one else, the fault is your relation to me. Which is to say that fault is mine. I think Yellow Tail means either to sever you from me or to have me think we're severed, which, in this isolation, would be no different. And the blade he intends is last Winter, which he must have gleaned I've been omitting in these many dispatches. And it is sharp enough, I fear, it still has enough fineness of detail in my memory that I can not even look at it directly, as my own. Yet there is agency, Claire. Perhaps even nothing else but agency.

As you know, or would, it was September when the Indian Agent for the Blackfeet arrived on the Reservation. His woolen suit yet had little rolls or balls of collected dander on the most unrubbed sections. His domicile was quaint and wooden and rustic and sufficient to his frontier post. Those are the words he would use in his painfully typed letters to describe it to his bride, at least. In truth the Agent's appointed living quarters showed evidence of a man having locked himself in its quarters for weeks at a time, as if hiding from his responsibility, or afraid of the unforgiving nature of Montana light in the months before the first snow. Andrew W. Collins III was that prior agent's name, a former cavalry officer released from military duty before attaining his zenith, for reasons unclear to his replacement. Had this post been a punishment for Collins? Or had he requested and been granted it, as it would ease relations between the Piegan and the cavalry, having a retired officer to mediate?

As with any new posting, there was much to learn that could have been shoehorned into no dispatch or charter, and, at the indirect suggestion of the Indian man already in employ to muck the stalls, this new Indian Agent made as his first order of business a grand tour of the Reservation.

It was September, so he had to wear his thick greatcoat, but there were times he folded it across the pommel of his saddle as well, to better drink in the unadulterated splendor spread out before him like an oil painting. The word the deputy commissioner had used to entice him West had been Edenic, and it was not an ill fitted term, but in his pride at being a representative of the federal government, this Indian Agent carried the biblical allusion farther, until, in his thinking at least, he felt himself to be the first man, an Adam on the plains, granting names to the antelope that seemed to hang suspended on air just beyond rifle shot, nodding to the deer bounding up from the breaks in the land he'd been told were coulees, a word which, in his heightened state of possibility, served him as an indicator that he belonged here, as it conjoined his French upbringing with his current posting. It felt like providence, he would have said in an early letter home, save that then he had still been confident his bride's father was yet reading over her shoulder, so had been tempering his romantic bent.

And the deer of course never failed, after running hard for a few lengths, to stop and look back at this Indian Agent, as if appraising his worth.

This of course he took as a show of respect, and allowed himself to think that as the deer felt, so would his Indian wards. He considered the likelihood that this posting, this land, these people, had all been minted for him and him alone, to prove his mettle.

And was he seeing the boy then already, from the corner of his eye? The boy throwing his featureless bird into the air time after time?

He no longer knows, Claire.

In the evenings of his first weeks on post, he would smoke on the porch with whatever Indians had gathered for handouts and then he would retire to his quarters to alternately study Collins' abandoned notes and to write his own, the first set for posterity, the second for delivery East, and written such that his distant bride would have no choice, in spite of his strict warnings, to journey out here.

And if she had?

Would she be buried on the Ridge with the rest now,

where the Indians still won't walk, as the lights have started gathering there on certain mild evenings, according to the men who yet watch?

But such pagan lights can not exist, of course.

And those first weeks of his post, the Ridge was not yet occupied. Then it had just been the last place west of the Agency that the wind passed on the way to his door, and the many chinks and orifices of his quarters. There were not yet six hundred people buried there.

God in Heaven.

His hands then were still clean, I mean.

A year later, though, sitting double on a horse with a man he didn't trust yet had no choice but to trust, one of his wards, in fact, his former wards, he would see that man smile so that the ice around his mouth would shift and crack, and he would ask this Indian Agent what he thought would be just recompense for last Winter, allowing of course that there were even anything owed in the first place?

This of course would be the way that particular Indian always framed things, such that to track back through them to the real meaning the Agent would become tired, and know it easier to simply accept the assertion than attempt any argument which might acknowledge the validity of that back path of reasoning.

Upon hearing this question, our Indian Agent would take it in and chew on it like a plug for a while. One he was by then familiar with. And then he would call forward to this Indian, as if only completing the joke, that if Heaven and Hell were to be excluded in this pagan land scape, as he suspected they would be, then perhaps the fitting equivalent to Hell for a white man would simply be to be forced to live life as one of his subjects.

It was intended only as a self deprecatory remark, of course, and said some what in mirth, and in anticipation of needing to escalate many removes above and to the side of whatever the Indian was going to propose. But then the Indian nodded, as if accepting this as an eventuality. As if this were an acceptable proposition, yes.

His next question was simply When? If this Indian Agent's just punishment for last Winter was to have to receive the charity he had been formerly and, the Agent had thought, generously bestowing, often times at great personal peril and sacrifice, then when might this spiritual apology best begin?

It was not a question the Indian Agent was expecting.

The obvious answer, of course, would be last Winter. Excepting that he was already there, or had been.

When the Indian Agent failed to answer, the Indian in front of him turned, asking the question again, as if this were not merely conversation.

At which point the Indian Agent, trying to safe guard himself, to save his soul for his estranged wife, said simply, and in the baroque Piegan counting he had acquired from doling what summer rations had arrived late, One hundred years hence.

But it was only conversation, Claire.

A person can not call down his own fate, even in trade, even in a language he knows but imperfectly.

Can he?

What I have not told Yellow Tail, though I suspect he knows, is that the boy across from me has the pallor and the supine posture of—

I've seen it a hundred times, Claire. Six hundred times.

He's starving.

This is what, with the rock, he was trying to avoid.

And but for the presence of his Indian Agent, he would have succeeded.

Just now I have held his head in my lap and stroked his forehead and prayed with a fervency I know is only allocated to the mad.

Yet his breath it rattles still, and his skin is cold.

Would that his Indian Agent would have let that feature-less black bird fly away, Claire.

Would that

six hundred other things.

But not six hundred and one.

Francis D.pere

Claire—

I am now sheathed in blood. It was warm. And it's not yet light, nor am I confident it will be again.

The blood is from Yellow Tail's horse. The one he informed me could have thin steaks removed from it and bear no permanent insult.

There are no such horses.

The boy, however, Lead Feather, in his sleep his jaws did worry the mouthful of meat the Indian Agent softened for him between his own teeth.

The rest of that steak, however, it flaps yet from the flank of a horse running into wall after wall of whiteness.

At least it screamed properly when the blade pierced it.

I don't think I could have endured its silence.

S.

Claire—

It is morning again, or afternoon, and Yellow Tail has yet to return.

As for the boy, he lives, though I know not how.

Perhaps in the stubborn way they always have.

I should not be here.

When I woke it took me long minutes to place myself in this dugout. The roof made no sense to me. That such a place could even exist. That I could be in such a place.

If it must be that I am still stumbling through yesterday's snow, lost, protracting my own death, insisting on its opposite, then it must also be that this letter is unwritten as well.

However, if that were the case—

I would need no pen, Claire, no faded journal to balance upon my knees.

And the boy, he would be risen already, smiling at me the way all these Piegan young do, as if I'm about to tell them the most humorous thing ever.

And there would be meat enough for everybody. Twice over.

Thanks Giving. It would be Thanks Giving.

If you could see me now, you would know that I am grinning, though not from pleasure.

There is water rising in my throat.

It is time.

—

By that first November, the Indian Agent for the Blackfeet had learned again how to swallow his own spit. It wasn't a thing he had ever given notice to before. But, as alone as he was, with none of his personal correspondence being answered and none of the Piegan talking to him, save the stable hand, the Indian Agent had become acutely aware of the rushing sound of swallowing that passed between his throat and his ear.

This is a measure of how empty his cabin was.

The days he was able to fill with his monastic duties, with the endless forms and copies of forms required by his post, and with cataloging the former Agent's voluminous though random notes, and with preparing the Agency grounds for eventual inspection, and with tending his horse as if for show or for sale—one of the prior Agent's notes claimed that the Piegan would judge a man by the quality of his horse—and with trying to document the births and deaths on the Reservation, and with trying to understand and appreciate the structure of the various bands and societies, and associate those bands and societies with camps that were already becoming permanent, would be hamlets in another decade, communities in a generation, towns for the grandchildren, and with more, for there is always enough with a federal posting to occupy the day. But it was the nights that troubled him.

By candle light, he fiercely desired the company of another human.

Making his way to the privy, the grass before him washed silver by the stars, he some times felt sure he was about to start falling up into the sky. And that if any Piegan were in the vicinity they would merely track his ascent until he was disappeared and then nod that the world was balancing itself back again. It would be just like their stories, of which the Indian Agent only had what fragments his predecessor had been able to smuggle out of lodges, crib onto his brittle paper and thusly forget.

For three days in late October, though, yes, the Indian Agent, or at least the Agency itself, had been the focus of everything in northern Montana.

The quarterly stipend of rations had arrived.

The Piegan were drawn from miles. It was the first accurate count the Indian Agent had been able to make, and, unlike their gatherings and ceremonies, this time they stood still and allowed themselves to be counted.

Moving with a deliberateness he had heretofore only attached to old men, the Indian Agent took the whole day dividing blankets up into even and evenly spaced piles, by household. And then to each pile he added flour and a modicum of the seed potatoes. The beef was still in the converted tack house, as the tack house was the only building on the Agency grounds on blocks. The intent had been to keep the rats from infesting it and gnawing the padding from the pommels, but such a store room was inessential now, as there was no longer a military detachment stationed on the Reservation. The Indian Agent simply kept his saddle beside his bed.

As for why the beef had been delivered in pallets instead of on the hoof, as had been the practice, the Indian Agent had been made to understand that it had to do with the cost of rail transport, and the unlikelihood of cold sides of beef being herded a few head at a time over the years into some side pasture. However, transporting sides of beef necessitated weather cool enough to accommodate such transport.

The summer previous, the decision had been made on behalf of the Piegan that their Winter appropriation of rations would be better preserved if quartered from August through until October. Aside from the coolness, which was the primary factor, there was also the added benefit that, by being forced to wait those few weeks, the Piegan might see the need for agricultural industry, and remember that need when the next growing season presented itself. A little hardship would forge their sense of community. And at the worst, they could simply do what they had been doing since time immemorial: hunt. There was always another buffalo or two if you rode enough ravines and kept your sailor's glass handy. To say nothing of the excellent fishing, if only these Indians could be convinced to fish.

In addition, there was of course the Indian's well known inability to conserve wealth. Give them their full rations in August and they would be hungry by November. Wait two months' time, though, until Winter has started to set in, reminding them of the need to ration their rations, a concept historically foreign to them, and their stores might very well last until the March installment.

However, the date agreed upon the summer previous as cool enough turned out to be unseasonably warm for northern Montana.

Flies had followed the pallets into the tack house.

The soldiers who delivered it had no explanation, nor any excuse.

Surely there were ways to prepare it though, the Indian Agent told himself, stacking blankets as slowly as possible, so as to dilate his good standing.

Did not the Indian famously make use of every part of the buffalo, and had not those buffalo lain all day in the summer sun more than once?

Perhaps it would merely be a matter of boiling long enough. The impurities would rise to the top to be ladled off, into the fire.

If necessary, he would even take the worst of it for himself, as a show of solidarity. Or blamelessness.

And at least there would be the blankets, and the flour, and the potatoes.

Right?

What else could I have believed, Claire?

Another way to say it, though, is how could I have so willingly believed my own lies.

But allow me if you will to remind you how alone with myself I was.

One's thoughts begin to feed upon each other in such a state.

I longed for you, or, in lieu of you, just some one to remind me I was alive. Some one to sit at a table with, or ride along side, even wave to as we passed in the street. For the Piegan have no such social customs. They acknowledge one another, of course, but in no way I can make sense of. I think it has something to do with the eyes, which are never looking directly into mine.

Collins has left no notes about this.

I understand him better for it, I think.

Being Indian Agent for the Blackfeet is a primer for death. You learn how to move as though invisible, as though you can have no immediate effect on your surroundings.

Meat, you want meat?

I can give you the ghost of meat, the carcass of food.

That night as the fires were sparking up, I made it known through Marsh that in the morning we would divvy up the rations. That this was New Policy.

Instead of assuming a central position and speaking loudly, Marsh instead sauntered from fire to fire, attending only maybe each third one, and when he relayed my words in the Blackfeet tongue it was as though he'd set them to a form of music. As if he were circulating a particularly well received joke.

When the Piegan men looked up to me after hearing the news that it would be morning, they would, to a man, smile, nod, and let their eyes move across me to the land behind me.

In the morning the fires were black smudges on the prairie, and the Piegan were all gone, with the blankets and the flour.

As the front door of the tack house had been left swinging, its crossbar broken in some quiet manner, the padlock still firmly affixed to it, there were now dogs in there.

The Indian Agent for the Blackfeet didn't chase them out.

When the stable hand returned the following week, the Indian Agent asked of him where had they all gone?

The stable hand had narrowed his eyes, either as if trying to remember or as if trying to translate his memory into the half English he could some times speak, if it meant standing instead of shoveling.

Any, the stable hand said, moving his mouth slow for the Agent.

Ainy.

To show, he pointed out, along the horizon, then, finally, lowered his head, made his hands into horns.

Buffalo.

In Collins' notes, *E'ini*.

Good, the Agent told him, good, but the stable hand shook his head no, leaned back into his spade, and couldn't be prompted into saying anything else, even when the Agent worked along side him.

That night, because he couldn't endure the sound of his own swallowing, the Agent instead spit into a tin cup, which he emptied by intervals into the stove.

It almost made it smell as if he wasn't alone.

The Indian Agent for the Blackfeet was mucking the ration meat out of the tack house when the post came from his superior.

Along with the usual claim forms was the reply he'd been awaiting. The rations were to be replaced. Further more, his superior, M. Sheffield, was to coordinate his annual inspection with the arrival of said rations, in order to supervise the Agent's growing rapport with the Piegan. Inevitable rapport were the actual words he used.

The Agent replied immediately and then whiled away the rest of the day in a long and wandering letter to his wife, a letter he finally deemed too lacking in focus to transcribe with the Calligraph.

That night the dog that had whelped her fourteen pups in the tack house returned to it again.

Because she was locked out of the tack house proper, she'd now wallowed out a place under the lee corner, and would raise her teeth if one drew near.

I have no idea what ever became of those pups, either.

But neither is this about them.

Three weeks in arrears of his letter, Sheffield was waiting at the stalls when the still green Indian Agent for the Blackfeet stepped out to survey the grounds.

That Sheffield could be there this early, and taking into account the snow that had been falling for the past three days without cease, the Agent knew that he, Sheffield, had to have his own rapport with one of the families camped down at the creek. Other wise he would have had no place to stay the previous night.

It made the inspection an empty formality, in a sense, as Sheffield must have already been informed as to the state of the reservation and the Agent's handling of Indian affairs so far.

Yet none of this mattered.

When Sheffield spoke the Agent's name across the twenty feet between them, it was the first time the Agent had heard it from another's lips in three months. He nearly cried. I say this honestly, Claire, and not to wound you. It's just important, if you hope to understand what I've done. What your Indian Agent is about to do here. What he's about to allow happen.

For most of the morning he's horseback with his superior, the two of them inspecting the various buildings in their various states of disrepair and incompletion, Sheffield's eyes lighting on the structures only for moments before inevitably flicking west, to the mountains, or back to the east, what the Piegan call their Sweet Grass Hills.

He tells the Indian Agent that this is the actual reason he's here. That what he likes to do is imagine that he's here before the white man, that he's the first one to be seeing all this.

A harmless fancy, no? he says, wiping his sleeve across

his lips to suppress an embarrassed smile. That he could be so vulnerable.

The Indian Agent understands.

To complete the idyll, no Piegan wander into the vista, so that the two of them do own the landscape for a few moments.

But then a bugle cuts through the morning chill.

Sheffield doesn't look around.

The Indian Agent does.

As always, the rations have been chaperoned to the tack house by a military detachment. The flag floats above the meat. Again, it's not on the hoof.

It's cold now, though, so that's of no concern.

And already Indians from the creek are wandering up from their lodges.

They can smell it, Sheffield states, touching his nose to show, then smiling.

The Indian Agent returns the smile, has been talked to in English all morning now.

On the return trip to the Agency grounds, Sheffield even inquired after you, Claire, as if this were a social call he was on, and so must make all the proper obeisances.

What I told him was that without your heart felt daily letters, I would not be able to endure.

It was no lie.

With the soldiers was Andrew W. Collins III, the Agent prior to myself. Whether military again or a civilian I still know not. He wore his old cavalry colors, though. They matched only imperfectly those of his detachment.

Where I found him was in the Agency house.

He was just standing there, taking account of all the small changes only he would be aware of.

My notes, he finally said.

I shook my head no but then realized I was standing behind him. Notes? I said.

They were in the second and third drawers on the right side of the wall desk. Instead of the alphabetical order I'd originally placed them in or the crude classification by content I'd attempted, they were now arranged simply by levels of coherency. My intent, I think, was to track his descent, and in so doing anticipate and perhaps even prevent my own.

It was no biography, though, and no confession. Towards the end it seemed more and more to be simply a catalogue of fears and irrational certainties.

Would that he had encountered Yellow Tail.

The reason the notes were in the only drawers that locked was that I did not wish to become infected.

They were for a book, Collins finally said, about the notes. A book I was going to write.

About the Piegan?

He didn't answer, had fallen again into reverie. Perhaps you become nostalgic for times you remember less clearly than other times, or for who you were then, I know not. But I left him to it, and to whatever of mine he wished to sift through.

Sheffield and the soldiers were appreciably better company. For the rest of that day, they were the extent of the civilized world for me, and I was loathe to let them go, to the point even of asking them to help me the following evening, when I had announced via Marsh that I would be doling out rations and supplies. My excuse for their requested presence was that I feared an uprising.

Looking back two months later, I would identify this as perhaps my first missed step.

But can you ever actually find it?

Perhaps it wasn't asking them to stay, I mean, but perhaps the kernel of that action was in taking in the landscape with Sheffield that morning, or perhaps it was that I had, secret even to myself, set myself up for such isolation, by relying only upon one person for correspondence. Rather I should have had acquaintances all along the frontier with whom to trade anecdotes and share revelations and whisper misgivings.

Or perhaps we never should have gone to that dinner at the Deputy Commissioner's.

However, I won't go back so far as to not follow you in the market that day, until your father's footmen apprehended me.

I've never been so satisfied to be caught. Because already I was trapped, just from seeing you select one fabric over another from a stall.

And this is what I do, isn't it?

Instead of telling you what immediately followed my actions, what effect my cause would ultimately have, I choose to dwell in fondness. To shirk my obligation, this task Yellow Tail has burdened me with. That I should unburden myself.

I told the soldiers to stay, Claire, yes. And Sheffield nodded his approval. And eventually Collins stepped out of his former living quarters and slit his eyes against the afternoon sun, saw me perhaps as a hazy shadow of a person, at least until he became adjusted to the light.

That night, amidst toasts, one of the men announced that the morrow would be Thanks Giving, and then Sheffield explained the holiday to us as Lincoln had in an address, and I looked out the window at the fires flickering to the west and nodded to myself.

Thanks Giving.

The Indian and the White Man together.

The pageantry spoke to me of civilization.

The following morn I woke to the aroma of meat roasting over a fire.

Collins looked up from his chair and explained to me that it was for the feast, for the holy day.

Stationed casually between the cooking fire and the Indian camps were the soldiers. Not watching but not not watching, either.

What Collins was sifting through, it seemed on a glance, were his old notes. I pretended not to have seen, though he obviously meant me to.

I washed my face and completed the rest of my morning ablutions, and by the time I became aware of proceedings outside, Collins had put away his book on the Blackfeet and resumed his old duties, grimly piling blankets and flour and what potatoes were left and, because this was to be the tenth ration, regardless of missing shipments, a pound of coffee. Added to that, because this was also to be the hundredth, were three pounds of beans and twice that in sugar. On to the top of each pile, then, Collins was also stacking, instead of the usual soda or tobacco, a single church hymnal. The hymnals were not treaty specific, so far as I understood, and I suspected they weren't rations at all, but had simply traveled the same route as the rations, and were actually intended for some fledgling place of worship.

But I didn't stop him.

Perhaps this would establish continuity for the Piegan, their old Agent punching the ration ticket for staples in the morning, the new Agent handing out the beef and pittance of bacon that night, both of them bending to their labors under the venerable aegis of their commander, their chief, Sheffield, who insisted upon the droll conceit of calling the Piegan by the name they use to refer to themselves, Pikuni, as if he were one of them, or could be.

The second misstep I took, Claire, it was less obvious, just felt in keeping with the last. But that of course is the way it always is, I know. Even unto death, as Pastor James used to say, right?

What I did was to allow the soldiers, whom I thought so far from home and thus needing a setting with which to anchor their spirits, I let them construct a crude long table upwind from the cooking fire, for us to celebrate Lincoln's holy day.

And, when Marsh was not to be found, Collins walked out into the camps and returned with two boys whom he seemed to know, or to know of any way.

One of them was the one who, two months later and until the ground thawed so they could open it, took it upon himself to keep the eyes of the dead closed.

Neither he nor the other boy had any English, but Collins had enough Blackfeet to direct them to the pots and the spits and the pitchers the soldiers had readied.

And thusly we ate, Claire, like men who had been starving. We fell upon the meat as animals would, and when I asked, Collins grinned and said the provisions were of course from the saddlebags.

But then Sheffield smiled, looked to the camp fires pale in the light of day.

Was it not the Indians who gave their own food so that the Pilgrims might live and eventually proliferate, though? he said.

He expected no answer.

And I wish I could say that the meat in my mouth began then to swell, Claire, but, you must understand. The tack house was stacked with meat. How could there not be enough? Could a Winter really be that long? And were not the Piegan acclimated any way?

And, regardless, Sheffield was right. For this Thanks Giving to be complete, as Lincoln intended, we at the table had to have reason to give that thanks, right?

When the Piegan drew close to the table, however, the soldiers made various adjustments to their posture so that it could be plain to all that the weapons of their daily life were, as always, at the ready.

And one of the boys ferrying food from fire to table was crying, yes, Claire, but did not Collins himself offer him a cube of meat? Perhaps he was the first Piegan of his family to be served domestic fare from an actual plate. It was an honor.

But I have no doubt you can hear the quaver in my voice, even through the pen and the tongues and the translator and the typewriters and the post and the years, and the unlikelihood of this ever reaching you.

What I try to do here, you see, is capture what I must have been thinking then.

Except I have to recreate it, as, now, from the darkness and the dampness and the chill of Catches Weasel's dugout, with Lead Feather expiring across the fire from me, it is difficult to even imagine the Agent I was before. The Agent I had to have been but a single year prior.

Eventually the holy day feast drew to a close, Claire, and, instead of allowing the Piegan the indignity of supping on the remains, the soldiers instead raked them to the dogs, who snarled and snapped and ate as dogs do, which is without chewing.

Think it'll be any different tonight? Sheffield said to me in jest, throwing his gaze out to the taciturn countenances of the Piegan, and he was my commander, Claire. Sharing a moment of joviality.

I smiled with him.

—

I am back again from standing outside in the wind.

Yellow Tail has still not returned.

What I was sure of, however, sure of beyond certainty, as if I had seen it myself but some how forgotten, was that there was another dugout within sight of this one, an old birthing hut or water catchment, large enough to hold three adult Piegan, if they wished to watch their Indian Agent's futile attempts to save one boy.

Is it some how culturally inappropriate for them to be in the same room when he stops breathing?

No.

Were that the case, the entire Piegan tribe would be carrying this proximal shame, after last Winter. After what I did to them.

If you want the reason I didn't pass out the meat that night as intended, it was because of shame, Claire.

With the soldiers there and with Sheffield watching and especially with Collins in attendance, and the sour judgements he kept always to himself, as if no longer concerned, or as if concerned solely with things of importance, I had no choice.

It was about discipline.

If a child misbehaves, should he not be chastised?

What had happened was, in the hours after our meal, when we had retired to my living quarters to smoke and trade stories and satisfactions, one of the blankets went missing from one of the piles.

Collins, as he had taken on the duty of the staples, was of course the one to alert us about the pilfering.

Since it would have been demeaning to myself, to my position of authority, to have to go lodge to lodge to discover this blanket, provided they weren't prepared for that any way, always passing the blanket one lodge ahead of me, and with Sheffield watching me, I exaggerated the action of shaking my head in disappointment, and then explained to Marsh that the meat, now, would be handed out the following morning. Provided none of the blankets or coffee or flour or beans or potatoes or sugar went missing as well.

At the point in my inflated monologue in which he began to understand what I was attempting to impart, and have him relay in my stead, he then looked into my face, as if sure I didn't know what I was saying.

But I nodded.

As I spoke to him, he was leaning on his Agency spade.

It was still standing there when he walked down to the camps, shedding along the way the clothes he'd been issued.

They always do that, Collins said, suddenly beside me.

What? I asked.

Act like it's the end of the world, he said.

No one had noticed that I had failed to include the hymnals in my list. It was supposed to be a kindness, a compromise, a message of my true and Christian intentions.

That afternoon, for supper, we ate another round of beef, and this time the soldiers didn't pretend that it wasn't from the tack house.

Every bite I swallowed of it, Claire, it is inside me yet.

The next wrong thing I did exactly one year ago today, if my reckoning is accurate, is that I didn't tend the fire.

While the soldiers actually had no slabs of meat in their saddlebags, they were able to collect a bottle or two and carouse into the night, finally burning even the table upon which we'd broken bread.

I watched from the porch with Sheffield.

Collins was anywhere.

At a certain point in the revelries, the bawdy songs and taunts thrown out into the darkness, we retired inside, Sheffield and myself.

The gunfire drew us back out, however.

It was deep in the morning, judging by the stars, and the soldier's bedrolls were strewn about the remains of the fire. There were no Piegan within sight, but evidently there had been.

In response, the soldiers banked the fire even higher, until its sparks trailed up into the sky and carried down to the creek.

Sheffield laughed and went back to bed but I stayed a few minutes longer, surveying the situation.

As I watched, a thin Piegan man unfolded himself from some cut in the ground I wouldn't have guessed was even there, and then continued his progress to the tack house.

Instead of calling the alarm, Claire, I smiled. You have to appreciate their tenacity, their will to live, their insistence upon survival.

But neither could I allow him free pass to more than his family's share of the meat.

When he stood for the latch, I whistled through my teeth.

He looked across the sleeping soldiers to me, then, and this is the Piegan character in sum, Claire, even while watching me watch him, his hand still rose steadily to that crossbar, so that I had to whistle again, harsher, so that one of the soldiers stirred.

Still, too, that Piegan, I never discovered which one, except that then he stood for all of them, and maybe was there with their approval, still he stared at me, as if it was he who was daring me.

When I stepped down from the porch, however, he turned to smoke, vanished into the darkness with a silence and sureness of foot that no white man has ever known, and I wish I could go on with this, Claire.

I want to so dearly.

But something about the boy, Lead Feather, lying across from me, his eyes open now but unseeing, as if in supplication, or indictment.

I have been lying.

The tack house and its store of rations didn't burn in a fire banked too high then left unattended, as I was leading you just now to believe.

There were gunshots that night, yes, but at no Indian in particular, just in warning, and revelry.

The other version I considered telling you, as it indicted the soldiers instead of carelessness, was that, their bottles emptied, two of the soldiers lured an Indian woman into the tack house on pretense of contraband rations for her family, but, once inside, shut the door and forced themselves upon her, so that, in the morning when I tried to hand out rations, none of the Piegan would take them, as the actions of the night before had tainted the meat, made starving the preferable course, as that only compromised the body.

But then you would have to have also believed that starving in mass was something they could have accepted, Claire. That it was on principle, that it was a chosen and agreed upon manner of death.

That's not the same people who stripped bark off the trees in hopes of living, though. That's not the same people who carried their dead out into the snow and fell with them and then had to be pried away.

What really happened.

I fear now that you must already know. That Sheffield has over the course of the summer maneuvered his way into your confidence at some social function, and informed you what exactly your husband was doing out West, on the frontier.

It's the only explanation I can conjure for your continuing silence.

On the chance that you know already, I will not even bother to dress it up for you as I'm wont to.

The morning after the eventless night a warm and unseasonal current drifted in from the east, so that the ground turned to mud, and we were all caked with it from the hips down, even Sheffield, who prided himself on the neatness of his appearance.

I presumed of course that the Piegan, sensing this warmth, would take immediate steps to salt and dry the meat I was about to deliver to them.

Except that, now, another blanket was missing.

I stared at the bereft pile for nigh on an hour, Claire, as if ready to convince myself that I had mistaken yesterday's pile for this one, but finally made it known to the Piegan that this meant now another day of waiting.

To enforce this, the soldiers garrisoned themselves around the tack house.

That day I ate little, and talked to no one.

The following morning, another blanket was gone.

It was a joke now, almost.

I shook my head in wonder.

The soldiers, while still guarding the meat, were now mostly on one side of it. On the other, the downwind slope, from my vantage point I could see a Piegan woman who I know wasn't Smokes in the Evening and wasn't Maleury, no matter that I insist on remembering each of them as there, I could see the woman reaching between the slats of the out-house with a branch.

She was bringing back tufts of meat and putting them in her parfleche, until it was bleeding.

At this rate, she would have a mouthful within the hour.

But then of course one of the soldiers stepped around the corner to relieve himself and caught her, and brought the butt of his rifle smartly into the side of her face, but I tried not to watch any of that.

Instead, her branch. It was still reaching into the tack house, as if she were still holding it.

When I turned away from it finally, Collins was sitting on the rail beside me.

It's getting too hot, I said to him. The meat's going to spoil.

You can't smell it already? he said, smiling with one side of his mouth.

They can still eat it, I said. They know how.

Collins shrugged, studied the fires.

So you're going to give in then?

It's for their own good.

Letting them take advantage of their Agent, you mean?

I didn't answer. There was no answer.

The next morning, as we'd come to expect, another blanket was missing.

The dogs were gathered around the tack house now. The same ones that had feasted last time. Perhaps this was Thanks Giving to them as well.

I wish there had been a fire, Claire.

Then maybe some of the meat would have been left intact, cooked.

Instead, six days later, days we measured in absent and unaccounted for blankets, the Piegan finally wandered away, leaving me to collect the flour and beans and coffee and sugar and potatoes and hymnals and what blankets remained, to save for them later, after the real snows.

In consolation, Collins assured me that to get another load of rations, all I had to do was fill out the right paperwork. Sitting over his old desk with me, he even showed me how to properly address it, thus cutting out as many of the intermediaries as possible. Because if the rations didn't come within the month—

He left that for me to complete. Which I did, Claire.

And the boy I just apologized to for that, he only stares, and has not been authorized to accept my apology.

Twice now he's stopped breathing, then caught his air again just when I thought it over and done with. As if he is under Yellow Tail's spell as well, perhaps. As if he awaits yet the completion of the story of last November, of the first

Thanks Giving to be celebrated on the Blackfeet Reservation, possibly in all of Montana.

Very well.

This.

On the morning of the tenth day, when the meat in the tack house was no longer in need of military guard, Sheffield and the detachment of soldiers excused themselves, and pointed their horses' heads back South.

I stood on the porch observing their retreat, already dreading my isolation, not knowing yet what the Winter held in store for me, and then Collins, who had been missing the entire morning, loped into formation.

As the cold had settled in again, the soldiers and Sheffield were of course bundled against it.

Collins was no different.

Except that, instead of Hudson blankets or military greatcoats or store bought buffalo robes, what he was wrapped in from the point of his chin to the tail of his horse was one of the ration blankets.

To be certain I saw, and understood, he looked back, his eyes glittering, and then reined his horse around, left me there, and there I remain, Claire.

Forgive me.

As always, your
Sam

Claire—

And so the Indian Agent returned his sheaf of antique papers back to the dugout's kindling stores, and pulled down grass and bark over the leather binding to assure it would be burned over the course of the Winter. Or perhaps it would be used in some ceremony or ritual to be performed over the boy's cold body, and in that way the Indian Agent could still be involved. And as Collins had said in one of his early notes any way, do not written words become prayer in their transubstantiation into smoke?

Even now the next supply of rations probably sits on a train so far away as to beggar imagination.

And so the Indian Agent bore witness to the boy's dying, and placed his hand to the boy's chest when the musculature spasmed and resisted the inevitable, the pain growing too intense, and in such a way did it infect him as well, so that he tore at his hair and his clothes and his face and renounced all he had once held dear, save the living memory of his distant wife. The hope of her.

And finally, in an effort he knew to be misspent, more childish than honest, an indulgence of sorts after a season of emotional penury, he stood from the dugout to trade himself to the storm, to offer himself in the boy's place, to insist upon it. He was then only in his shirt and leggings, as preparation would only have served as acknowledgement of the futility of the deal he meant to strike.

His teeth were set for the wind to take him, his eyes already slit against the stinging snow, but none of it came.

The storm had abated.

The large flakes were falling almost straight down now, and so thickly it was as though he could hear their thousand individual, padded landfalls, like an inarticulate whispering, a susurrant aerial murmur.

And more.

A breathing. A huffing.

It was the federal cattle he and his tribal guide had ridden through two days previous. The government cows, as the Piegan termed them. The cavalry beef. The untouchable food.

The Indian Agent regarded them. Their frozen hides and tired eyes and nostrils flecked red from breathing ice for so many days already.

Perhaps they'd been drawn to the heat from the dugout.

But perhaps not.

This wasn't the same Indian Agent from a year ago.

Thanks Giving, he said aloud, as if naming this feeling of certainty, this suddenly holy day, then, nodding to himself as if to stop would be to question his decision, he stepped half back into the dugout for the left behind rifle he'd not written about yet, as he thought it best his wife not know his suspicions as to why that rifle had been left behind.

It was a single shot. A ball gun, with a brass tipped horn hooked from the hammer lock.

The Indian Agent wadded and packed and set the flint, and kept his hands slow so as not to spook the government cows.

They were beyond that, though.

The Indian Agent settled the long octagonal barrel between the eyes of the closest cow.

She looked along the rusted steel barrel, back up at him.

Maleury, he whispered to her, intoning it just as reverently as his tribal guide did—it was the most powerful word he knew—and then he shot her, and when she wouldn't keel over, he leaned into her with his shoulder and then pounded on her with all his weight and finally, with a great exhalation, she died, her eyes and nostrils packing themselves with snow.

The Agent stared at her for as long as he dared, then tamped the rod down the barrel again, shot the next government cow, and the next, and the one after that, and this is the only way to harvest life in great numbers. Where you have to stop between each, to consider, and to acknowledge what it is that's being given to you, and to offer thanks. It was a thing the guide had mentioned once while looking far away into the past, at Marias, just before his smile flickered back onto his face and he told the Indian Agent about the days after the massacre, when the elk family sought to apologize for the soldier's actions, to restabilize the world, not by angling their long horns at the cavalry and running them through, but by letting the guide use their own bodies as shelter.

The proof of that sacrificial act, the guide said, was that he was here, a product of the elks' compassion.

Except that was the same proof he had offered for his horse, which he claimed to have eaten many desperate steaks from.

But none of that mattered right now.

The Agent counted as he moved among the cattle, and

at the end of it there were twenty four beeves splayed around the dugout, and he was clumped with their warm blood, so that he had to look at his own arms to be sure they were yet his.

And this was only the first part.

The second part was to lower himself to the first one he had dropped, and cut out her tongue by the base, as it was to the Piegan a coarse delicacy.

In the dugout, because there was no time to boil it, the Agent seared the tongue in the embers then cooled it in the snow and then worked it into his own mouth and turned it to paste, to medicine, and passed it with his hand to the boy, who sucked blood from it as an infant, insensible, and perhaps the cattle had been unhindered long enough, left alone on the Blackfeet grass, that the tongue over which that grass passed tasted even of buffalo, and woke some dormant memory which the rock had pushed too deep into the boy.

And so the boy ate the rest of the tongue, down even to the base, and the next also, and only rolled over when the third was presented.

The Agent watched him sleep.

It looked like no more than that.

But then the door flapped in, reminding him of his trade, of what he had done to keep the boy alive.

Again he stood from the dugout, this time in his boots and makeshift jacket, yet still the wind cut to his core, taking his breath. The storm was hungry.

The Agent was no longer alone either.

Standing a hesitant distance from him were his guide and the boy's parents. Across the back of the horse that had found the guide in the storm was the antelope that had run almost to the third lake over the last two days.

But now the antelope was less vital.

The government cows.

The guide looked to the Agent for evidence of this crime, or explanation, and the Agent only opened his eyes over all the beef, said in the French in which it sounded better, Pour Vivre.

To Live is what it meant.

Rations.

And neither had to say aloud that the next time the soldiers came up now, they would be leaving with the Agent in chains. Not for killing the six hundred Piegan, but for slaughtering the twenty four government cows. For it was an action that would become legend, and Sheffield had agreements with a few families. And the Agent would not deny it any way.

All of this the guide could see in the Agent's eyes, and so he rolled the antelope off his horse and offered the ropes to the Agent, in trade for what the Agent was giving them.

The Agent took the ropes with a finality, and wound them about his hand in thought but then rose up onto the horse and surveyed the Indian land all around him, and finally settled not on the Sweet Grass Hills to the east, but on the Back Bone of the World, the mountains to the west, somewhere through the storm.

And so it was decided.

The guide held onto his lips and said nothing, though he knew the storm was gathering up there, and that that Agent would be dead within two days. Unless of course the old four leggeds up there took pity on him as they had once for the guide, and offered to hold this Agent inside for however long the storm lasted, carrying him in their bellies as their own young even, for generation upon generation.

And then the guide smiled, for he knew this was so.

And so he looked up again to the Agent, who nodded and spurred the horse that needed no spurring, but then after a few steps the Agent stopped and turned sideways against the wind.

Standing now at the mouth of the Earth Lodge, wrapped in his mother's star blanket, was the boy, and though he refused yet to smile, yet he stood as if untouched by the wind and held the eyes of the Agent, and finally said the name of the Agent's wife. This made the Agent close his eyes, open them again, staring at no one. Then, shaking his head like everybody knows he does, as if in agreement with himself, he reached deep into his shirt, for a folded piece of his paper with the writing on it he insisted upon, even when the guide had pled with him to conserve his meager energies.

The missive was still warm from his chest, and had been rubbed with liniment to preserve it.

After touching it to his mouth, the Agent handed it down to the guide, who took it as he had been taking the rest and held it up as if to ensure delivery, and then the Agent straightened himself atop the horse, which had no sign of injury on its flank, and then this Indian Agent man rode away from his first federal posting, and was never seen again.

Francis Dalimpere
Indian Agent for the

BLACKFEET.

In big white letters, on every windshield in Browning.

Like we needed reminding.

God.

Not that I wouldn't have been there with everybody else. It was the first time we'd made regionals since my middle uncle was a senior.

He was probably there too, even.

It's basketball, after all.

But then, in the stupid way things work, the game came to us.

Doby Saxon, his face bloody like always, his eyes drunk, his dumb fingertips dribbling the ball into the concrete, half the time hitting it on the outside of his foot and having to chase out into the grass after it.

I was the last one in Browning to see him that night,

yeah.

My stupid little brother would say it was him, but he wasn't standing at the front window, he didn't see the way Doby was running at first, like away from something, or into something else, my dad's six-pack tucked up against his side, but then he lost his breath not even all the way to the road yet and just bent over there.

For a long time I didn't think he was getting back up.

The bandage I'd tied on his hand was already coming off.

It was probably from one of their idiot games, him and Robbie. Who can punch through this windshield first? Who can touch that lightbulb the softest? What if I put rocks in my hand and *then* squeeze the bottle?

What my mom says about them always is that their friend's only just waiting for them, and that it won't be long either.

She's wrong though.

Not that Jamie isn't waiting, and not that Robbie can live very long, but Doby, God.

I don't know.

Some Indians don't know how to die, really.

Like, if we'd had just a line of Yellowtails like him two hundred years ago, it'd be all different now. Because it's only funny to them, getting hurt, using themselves up so fast. And then the ones that try, that matter, like my middle uncle, the one my brother was named after—Jet, not Step—all it takes is one good tap, one bad night, and bam, it's over, done with, goodbye and get out the chalk.

What my mom says about him when she'll say any-thing is that he's family. It's like she's just reminding herself, though. If he got to the game that night, I mean, it wasn't with my mom and Yvonne, guaranteed. She'll even go all the way out to the Conoco just to duck him, and then pretend she just wanted to talk to Danetta at the counter, something stupid like that.

But now last week they boarded the windows of that one up early.

Maybe we'll go back to horses for the winter, since they don't run on unleaded.

And it's not like me and Little Step don't give our middle uncle candy bars and stuff. And he knows who we are too, and Step's not even afraid of his caved-in face anymore, and he's a hero anyway.

Just nobody knows it.

What my dad says about him is only half in words. The rest is with his eyes, biting his lip and looking at some orange rim from forever ago, then squinting, saying Jet, god*damn*. The boy had a shot that would make you cry, that would always make everybody in the gym just hold their breath and wait, even the ladies selling fry bread who never watched, even the coaches who'd been doing this forever already, even the cheerleaders for the other team.

When his voice gets floaty like that, he's talking about my mom's brother, sure, my middle uncle, but he's not only talking about him either.

My brother Jet could play too, see.

It's why we've still got the concrete slab in back of the house, and the regulation goal.

Because Jet was supposed to be our uncle all over again.

But then there were Doby Saxons in his grade too. There always are, I guess. And they always skate out just a minute or two before the sirens, then laugh about it until next time.

It's a trick my middle uncle finally learned.

And I'm not supposed to know it either, but I do.

It's why he smiles now. Why I know he made it to the game that night.

Our star player, 34, he's the new Jet. Nobody calls him that—his name's too Indian, too cool, all one word like they spell it now—but I know the real story of it, I saw my uncle after...I saw my uncle after he did it, and lived.

Where he spent the rest of that month was in the old coop behind our house, that's too high for the dogs to get into, too low for the horses to stick their heads in, and just right for the wind.

What he was doing, mostly, was singing to himself. Songs I didn't know, and still don't.

When I finally followed them back to him, though, he just nodded to me, smiled, and closed his eyes, satisfied, and that was how I started putting it together.

A few weeks before, 34, who mattered, his kidneys had started quitting.

Already then my middle uncle had been watching him practice, watching him shoot. Rising onto the balls of his feet when 34 drifted up into the air, and pulling his lips away from his teeth so he could suck in breath, control the ball's arc, nod when it kissed off the glass with a new spin.

But then, like my brother, like my middle uncle, the world was already trying to pull 34 back down, so that a Doby Saxon or a Robbie Cut Nose could leave him in the concrete tipi one Saturday night, like they never even knew him.

Jet still had a few moves, though.

The first one was to find one of 34's burnout nephews who was already older than 34, but stupider too, still celebrating his birthday from last week, then the next was to flag that nephew down in the middle of the day, with a full bottle that caught the sunlight just right, splintered it across the whole reservation. After that, it was cake, they just went on Indian automatic pilot, so that that first bottle turned into two more, then a case, then a trip over to St. Mary's for the good stuff, if they could just get there before the white guy who lived in that trailer got back from picking up his sister down in Great Falls, something stupid like that.

My middle uncle probably even put the five dollars of gas in 34's nephew's tank for him, and paid for it himself.

Because they were going to need to go fast for it to work.

When he went inside to pay, that was the next part.

What my middle uncle did was call the ambulance, say that he'd just come over from St. Mary's, and seen a car belly-up out in the pasture, the tires still spinning.

Before they could ask anything else, he hung up, maybe touched the place in his face that was all dented in.

And then, not even saying goodbye to Danetta or anybody, he went back to 34's nephew's car, pulled the door shut behind him and nodded ahead with one finger, and they were gone, flying like all Indian cars can, only bottoming out when it didn't matter, making every turn even, the radio screaming, my uncle holding onto the mirror outside his door, studying himself in it and finally nodding, then turning like to look for another beer in the backseat but unaccidentally pushing the steering wheel too far over in the process, so that they lost the road, cartwheeled out into the pasture, breaking over three of the five white crosses that were already there.

The ambulance screeched up while the tires of the car were still spinning, even.

I know because my middle uncle watched them from the tall grass, his hair bloody, his leg broke in two places and maybe his collarbone too, then he watched them leave, to deliver 34 the kidney he needed, that everybody knew he needed, even stupid Robbie Cut Nose, who wanted to be a hero too that night, or at least to not be Cunt Nose anymore.

He was too late, though.

My middle uncle was already crawling through the fields and the pastures to our chicken coop, for me to find, and start bringing candy bars to.

He's the reason we made it to regionals, the reason that every windshield in Browning said BLACKFEET, that the radio that night had even cut into its own request hour for the game.

Only nobody can know it.

I can see my middle uncle as he must have been that night though, not in the bleachers with everybody else, but standing with his hands in his jacket pockets down by the baseline, against the shiny brick, and rising up onto his toes each time 34 lifted for a shot, and for as long as that goddamn ball's in the air, I know, he's Jet again. For all of us.

And if anything else matters, I don't know about it.

We heard what he was doing out at Starr School. That if we hit him going sixty, it wouldn't even be our fault.

Phone had already gone back to Alice's by then, but Luther still had his aunt's Caprice. He slid the keys across the roof to Dally and we were gone, Luther at the wheel, and even before we got all the way to the first of the house lights for Starr School, we already had the Caprice straddling the yellow lines, so Doby could know.

Luther wanted to turn the headlights off—it was still a joke to him, I think—but Dally shook his head no. That we needed to be just anybody else to Doby, and to anybody watching from their windows.

It needed to be an accident, he meant. A suicide.

It's exactly those kind of details that keep you out of jail.

I just sat in the backseat, so I had a straight-on view of Doby Saxon rising from the asphalt. Just a soft-edged shadow at first, but then getting sharper, and sharper, and not moving.

How much he owed Dally for last weekend was sixty dollars, for a twenty-five-dollar bag that wouldn't have pulled fifteen anywhere else but on the reservation on a Saturday night. But this wasn't really about the bag. It was for Jamie, Dally's cousin.

Dally locked his elbows against the dash.

That was how I knew we were serious this time.

"Luther," I heard myself say, and his eyes flicked to me in the rearview but the Caprice never wavered.

"Shit," Dally said through his teeth, and then Doby was almost on the hood, and I was screaming, I think, because I knew he was coming through the glass at me, but somehow Dally's arm had unlocked itself from the dash, hooked its hand onto the outside of the steering wheel.

The Caprice shuddered over, its weight wrong and sluggish, and it only spun Doby around.

In the moments after him, we were weightless, floating through a stand of mailboxes, Luther fighting the wheel, never even making a sound, just staring hard and mad at the fence coming up to meet us.

It never did, though.

Like every night, the Caprice slung its ass to the other side of the road, skidding gravel out into the night, and then straightened up.

Dally was screaming too by then, but it wasn't the same as mine.

He was slamming his palm up into the headliner, like this was a ride we were on.

Instead of slamming on the brakes, too, Luther just kept coasting, finally looked over to Dally for an explanation.

"Posterity," Dally said, nodding down one of the Starr School roads, to where all the houses were.

"His or ours?" Luther said.

Dally shook his head at this, smiled, and said "A *camera*, man. Twice can push the button just right before—"

He finished with his hands, so that Doby Saxon exploded against the front of the Caprice.

Luther smiled, liked it, and we cut back to Browning for a camera, but never could find one that worked, until Luther remembered Chris.

She'd bought one special for the game, had had it in her purse all week.

It was an hour later before we finally figured she was out in Starr School, already spending the night with Gina.

"Look," I said, trying to point with my chin back into Browning, anywhere but Doby, but Luther and Dally were already set.

We pulled the Caprice right up to Gina's window, then Luther got out, spit on his finger and rubbed a circle into one of the panes until it squealed, but then Dally saw where Chris was: sitting out in the weeds, hugging her knees.

Luther looked to us, telling us to stay there, and then went to her.

They'd been together on and off for two years already.

It took him almost twenty minutes to talk her back to the Caprice.

"What about Gina?" Dally said, holding the door open for Chris.

"Sleepyhead," Luther told him, and lowered himself into the front seat.

It was me and Chris in back now, and she'd been crying.

Before backing out, Luther got up again, reached into Gina's uncle's Grand Marquis for Chris's purse.

He came back flashing the camera, and handed it like a playing card across to Dally, who just wound it, passed it back to me.

"What for?" Chris said.

"You'll see," Dally said, and Luther fishtailed out of the yard, leaving the trailer shrouded in dust.

Instead of coming from the game, the way everybody else was, this time Luther backed up to get a running start from the west, and turned the brights on.

Chris leaned forward, her hands digging into the seats.

"Luther—" she said, her voice already going shrieky, but we were almost there.

"Now!" Dally called out to me, and I fumbled the camera up with Chris looking to me, confused, and then Luther whispered shit and hung a tire over into the ditch, slipped past Doby Saxon a second time.

A quiet mile down the road, where Doby wouldn't be able to make out the brake lights, we pulled over.

Before Dally could say anything to me, Chris was attacking Luther, kicking the seat with her track legs so that he couldn't even turn around right.

I finally wrapped my arms around her, held her down to the seat.

Both doors opened then, and the bench seat folded forward.

Chris was still screaming, and kicking from the knee down.

"She doesn't want you to do it," I said through her hair.

"Good thing we weren't asking her then," Luther said back.

"What's she even care about his sorry ass for?" Dally added.

I let her go, stood from the other side of the car, breathing hard but not just from holding her.

A silver truck slashed by, giving us a lot of room.

Dally watched them gone then cut his eyes back to me.

"You with her then?" he said.

"What?"

"You didn't push the button, Twice." He held his hands in the shape of a camera, to show what he was meaning here.

"Tim would have," Luther said.

I looked over to him, didn't look away.

Tim was my brother.

"Fuck that," I said to them both. "It's just Doby Saxon."

"Exactly," Dally said, and Chris collapsed to her knees.

"What the hell?" Dally said to Luther, like Luther was responsible for her.

"I can take the picture," I said to them, and Chris finally looked up, still crying but not so loud.

"What?" Luther said to her.

She shook her head no though, just stood, and then we all saw it.

In her right hand somehow was the camera we needed.

"Chris," Luther said, but it was too late.

Chris Cut Nose turned, flitted away into the night like a deer, cutting across the pasture back to Browning, maybe, her feet not making any noise at all.

Without even meaning to, I fell in, leaving Luther and Dally behind finally, and after the time when my lungs caught on fire then went out again, I realized that Luther had been right. I wasn't like Tim at all.

Instead of really running after Chris, I was running with her, and wasn't going to stop until I had to.

She found me at the game in Butte, first quarter, and I didn't even remember her. She was all the way from Standing Rock. The same way there were some Sioux that got on the Blackfeet rolls wayback, some of us had snuck over the line too, got counted wrong on another rez, just never told anybody.

"You're Junior," she said, and I looked over.

She was a kid.

"See that guy out there?" I said, nodding to 34.

"You're Junior," she said again.

"He shouldn't even be alive right now," I went on.

This time she didn't say anything, until I looked back around to her during an out-of-bounds.

Then I had time to remember her, smile.

"You're Valanna's kid," I told her.

"I don't remember you."

"Then how'd you find me?"

She pointed to Sidney in the stands, who was like a bible on the reservation. She knew who begat who and pretty much exactly how back for about six generations.

"And how'd you know to ask her?"

"She saw me."

"Probably help if you didn't look just like your mom."

"Sorry."

The story of me and Valanna goes back to when I used to dance. But I haven't broke out my bustle now for years. It'd probably crack even, if I tried.

Valanna had danced too, traditional.

Her daughter was about three feet taller now than she'd been then, though. And about half dangerous.

"So he just has a number, no name?" she said about 34, and I smiled, rubbed my lips with the side of my hand.

The score then was 18 all.

"Kid Nee," I told her, smiling.

"Mom said you were funny, yeah," she cut back.

"Where is she?"

"Mom?"

"Valanna. I haven't said that name…shit. I mean—"

"Don't worry. She works nights now."

"And just lets you go all over America?"

"Not exactly."

And then I knew.

Any reservation you pick, the girls all have to run away at a certain age. Only, in this case, the girl was coming home. Sort of.

I blew some air out my nose.

"I'm not supposed to ride with strangers though," she said.

"And what am I?"

"Mom liked you." She shrugged—24 to 20 somehow—then turned around backwards, leaned on the rail so she could study all the Blackfeet faces in the stands. "Anyway, I can see the future, yeah?"

"The future?"

"I know you're safe."

"It's not me I'm worried about."

"Your white wife."

"My wife, yeah."

"She doesn't have to know. All I need's a ride."

"Shit."

"Look at it this way. What if I ride back with some drunk Indian and die?"

"You're Valanna all over, know that? Serious though, my wife'll kill me if I—"

"—if you help an Indian girl get back to her reservation? How white is she?"

I didn't answer, just watched us go down two more points.

"*My* music," I finally told her. "The whole way."

"Not country, is it?"

"Maybe."

"How far is it? To walk I mean?"

I had to smile then, lower my head.

At half time I bought her a coke and a bag of popcorn, then she disappeared and I thought that was that, was able to concentrate on the game, on 34 turning it on in the fourth quarter like we all knew he would, like we would too if we had his talent, and one time, even, racing for a lost ball, having to walk the sideline like a tightrope before turning on the speed, pulling up for a short jumper nobody was expecting, off the glass even, so that the bottom of the net just spit it out at the ground, he was only about six feet from me, and what I wanted to do for some reason was reach out and touch him. Just on the shoulder or the arm, I don't know. It doesn't make any sense. But that's the way he made us all feel too, that season. Like Indians again.

It was stupid, I know.

But I still wish I'd reached out that night, over the rail.

On the way to my truck I stopped at Lonnie's to fill my coke cup with some of his famous coffee. He was pouring whiskey in his, but all I needed was coffee, thanks. Jeannie would smell anything else on my breath, and anyway, even without her, I was different now. Clean.

I never would have guessed it either.

Go to enough sweats though, and the music kind of gets inside you somehow, until you're thinking in those beats.

I don't know.

I just wove through the parking lot to Jeannie's car, was all the way to the edge of town before the girl sat up in the backseat.

I clamped onto my cup hard enough that the coffee ran down over my fingers, made little rivers down into the defroster, so that it was going to smell like caffeine in the morning.

Part of it was the surprise, sure, but a bigger part was that, for a moment, I thought it was Valanna. That I was going to have to choose now between her and Jeannie, when it was Jeannie who saved my life every day of the week.

But could she dance like Valanna?

I angled the rearview down to see the girl better.

"Where to then, ma'am?" I asked, shaking my head, trying not to smile too much.

"Home, James," she said, her lips all pursed up.

"It's Junior," I told her, and she smiled with her eyes, said it again, "Home," and I nodded, put it on a country station.

"Thirty-Four," she said after a while, "it doesn't sound like an Indian name."

"What about Junior?" I said.

"That's very Indian, yes," she said. "Very creative."

"And Jeannie?"

She shrugged.

"Valanna?" I asked.

"Sounds like a bologna product."

"I'll tell her that when I call her tonight."

"You won't."

I shrugged.

"Your wife won't let you," she added.

I shrugged again, and with a flick of her eyes four hours later she directed me north of Browning.

"Why not Thirty-*Five*, I mean?" she said finally. "Wouldn't that be like one better?"

"You liked the way he played, yeah?" I said back, repositioning my rearview on her response, like I was cupping it in my hand, was going to save it, and that was the reason she saw it first.

Not black cows in the road or a car stalled right in front of us, but a flashing out in the pasture.

Like somebody was taking a picture out there.

Of us?

I let my foot off the gas, said it: "What the hell?"

Twenty seconds later it was a girl, the Cut Nose girl who's a Sainte too, and so can run forever.

She had a camera in her hand, was holding it ahead of her.

I stopped and she popped the passenger door open, fell in, nodded ahead, fast.

"Get my good side," I told her holding my chin up for the next picture, and she looked over to me for a long time then finally smiled, let herself start breathing hard like she needed to.

"Where to then?" I said for the second time that night then, which was about twice more than ever before.

"Gina's," she said, still out of breath.

"Wallace's girl?"

Chris nodded and I eased forward, only just remembering that I somehow had Valanna's daughter with me too, after all these years.

In the rearview, what I could see of her at first was how she was studying Chris, but then, because she'd never been here before I guess, she looked back out to the pasture, to see what other Indians might be out there too, running for our car, and, just like when Doby Saxon had walked into the diner, I looked where she was looking too, and half on accident said what I'd said then in Indian, which was just thank you, but bigger, like an offering too.

Without turning her head, Chris nodded, and, from the backseat, Valanna smiled and said that that was his name then, yeah? Thirty-Four, what I'd just said?

I looked back to her, trying to make it last, this stupid joke, but before I could figure out how to say 34's name in Blackfeet, Chris's hand clamped down on my wrist, harder than any fifteen-year-old girl should be able to.

We were about halfway through Starr School then.

When I told Malory about it through the glass, her face didn't even change at all at first. Because she's Malory. She just nodded, let her eyes slide past me, to the other visitors lined up to see their inmates.

Since Mom had gone last weekend, this was my turn.

How long Malory was still in for depended on her pretty much, the judge said.

It was another way of saying forever.

By the time the casino bulls caught Malory that night, she'd tumped over a money cart. The reason they charged her with grand larceny instead of just drunk and disorderly like usual, or even destruction of property and fleeing the scene and resisting arrest and assaulting a police officer, was that two of the tourist quarters from the money cart got stuck in her shoe. They showed up on the metal detector at the jail. So, fifty cents for her meant seven more years tacked on, because she was robbing from a casino instead of just a person. This is what it's like to be Indian in Montana.

What I was telling her, too, it was about Doby.

I was crying, I guess. Just because I can remember when she had him and he was was going to be perfect like they're all going to be, and better, and never have anything bad happen to him.

It's the same thing I thought when I had Chris, I know. My first girl. My second chance.

But she never went up onto any mountains with her dad, or had one of her friends die right there with her, or any of the rest of it, I already can't remember it's been so much with him.

And her dad wasn't a Yellowtail either, there's that.

Not that I would ever say that to Malory.

What I told her was just cut and dried, pretty much the way Chris told it to me when I picked up her film for her, asked her if that was who I thought it was?

At first she pretended like she didn't know what I was talking about, but I used to be fifteen too.

She'd been out there that night after the game, at Starr School. Not just at Gina's like she said, talking on the phone, being stupid. Instead, she was being the kind of stupid I had been. Except I'm not going to let her wind up like me. Even if it means locking her up every night, making her train until that's all she knows, to run, and to keep running.

You've got to try, I mean.

But Malory knew all that already.

What she didn't know was about her son, that she'd traded herself for that night, just so he could get away.

It worked.

That's the first thing I tell her when I sit down, that it

worked, that he got away, Mal. But then I'm laughing and crying both at once and Malory's just waiting for me to be able to talk again.

You'd think the state would have tissue boxes, but they don't care.

This is the way it happened.

Chris was in the car with Junior, who wasn't even drinking or anything. She'd been out running because she'd eaten two fry breads at the game and three cokes, wanted to sweat it out like she usually did, and it wasn't too cold or anything, and she doesn't care about that anyway, because you can't.

But anyway Junior saw her, picked her up, and then was going too fast on that road by Starr School, because who can know, right? You can't expect Indians to be jumping out from around every tree and every rock. You'd never get any place that way.

And he was saying something in Indian too, Junior, or it sounded Indian, but Chris wasn't listening, and it was lucky that he'd picked her up too, because he wasn't even paying attention to the road at all really, so that when Chris grabbed onto him to stop he just did, without looking, and the car he was driving that night, Jeannie's, it was maybe two feet from Doby's legs, or closer, so that they couldn't even see his knees anymore.

He just stared at the car, and everybody was quiet.

"That better not be anything dead," Junior whispered then, about what Doby was carrying, "or alive either," he added, right before some headlights popped up behind them, Doby looking over the roof of Jeannie's car into them, then down to Chris, his cousin, who he just nodded at, like they knew a secret, and the next part, the way Chris tells it, it's just that Junior leaned out the window and told Doby he could have a ride too if he wanted, Jeannie's car was a taxi that night, what the hell, but the way Junior tells it, it's all different. The way Jeannie says Junior tells it is that Chris, and you know how quiet she is all the time, it's why she does track I think, she had the door opened before the car even stopped, and stood into the coming headlights only just for a split instant before diving for Doby, dragging him around to the side of the car, pushing him hard into the backseat before he could even fight.

At which point Junior said something else in Indian, about Doby. Because maybe it was the first time he'd seen him since he came down out of the Park that time covered in blood, and now Doby was bleeding again.

Either way, the car that was coming, it swerved to miss them, clipped a mailbox instead and then just kept going.

Chris sat there like she was cold all of the sudden and nodded to herself, watching the car's taillights kiss each other gone, then she slumped down in the seat to get warm and Junior pulled away, only, when he started to turn down the road to Wallace Kills First's place, Chris shook her head no, just nodded ahead, out past Starr School, wherever, it was still too early, and Junior was just the driver that night and lived that way anyway so he shrugged, kept going, looking in the rearview for Doby, sitting by that other girl that Chris didn't even know. And they weren't saying anything, were just riding and riding, waiting to get to East Glacier or St. Mary's probably, until they drove into some snow, just the slow and heavy kind that wasn't even going to build up really, which is about when Chris says she looked into the backseat but still didn't know the girl, and this time it was Junior who put on the brakes himself, locked the tires up.

Running across in front of them like ghosts except heavy

enough to make the road shake, were thirty or forty elk, close enough that they were having to jump over the hood of the car, and one even went right over the roof, until Junior said to Doby without looking in the mirror that he was a Yellowtail, right?

Doby nodded, Chris said—you could just tell—and Junior nodded back, said not to say anything then, and started in on a story Earl had told him once that his dad had told him, that was from his dad before, from the bow and arrow days, and Junior probably wasn't even lying about having heard it from Earl, because Junior didn't always not drink, right?

The story, too, it was a joke mostly, like all of Earl's stories, was that one time an elk had found a white man lost and dying in the storm, and they'd talked to each other, and finally the elk, because it knew the man needed to live, to be warm, it took pity and laid on its side and let the man cut it open and crawl inside, and stay warm like that even though the snow piled up all around them for days and days and even years, only when the man finally crawled out again, everything was different, because that elk you crawl into, it's not the same one you crawl back out of, right?

"An elk," the girl in the backseat said then, leaning forward instead of laughing, "like these you mean?" but Doby was already shaking his head no, like he was in a dream here, and had been for a long time already.

"It was a moose," he said then, for the first time since it happened I guess, and he was maybe crying just in his voice a little but Chris says she doesn't think he even knew it. "He was—the moose laid down right in front..." And then he held his hand out to show the moose like he'd seen it too, like *he* was the white man in that joke, then nodded, said "Dad always, always was saying—" but didn't finish it, caught his lips together instead, like remembering that he didn't talk about Earl anymore, at least not out loud.

And Junior didn't say anything stupid like he usually does, he just held the wheel until Doby settled his voice down again to say about the elk that they were from the Park, yeah? And that's where you can see the Yellowtail in him the most, I guess, from that criminal hope in his voice, but that's not the end either.

The end is what finally even made Malory Sainte make a fist of her hand, that she isn't going to let go of for a long time, for the whole rest of her time probably.

It was the girl.

In the picture Chris turned around and took, the last one on that roll, the girl's sitting close enough to Doby in the backseat that the sides of their hands are touching like they know each other, like it was a date they were on, and what she was saying to him about the elk right then was that he was going to shoot them all, wasn't he? Bam, bam, bam.

Doby smiled his dad's smile, that he was caught but didn't care either, and looked over to her, careful not to move his hand that was touching hers, and asked how she knew that?

"I can see the future," she said, shrugging because it was such a normal thing to be able to do, or because she was lying, and Junior started to pull away some but Chris was still holding her breath to listen.

"Yeah," Doby said, laughing through his nose like he does.

"Really," the girl said, "clairvoyant. It means sees clear. Real Indian name, yeah? Sees Clear. Runs Fast. Two Dogs Fu—"

"*Whitelk*," Junior interrupted, his eyes a little hot in the rearview, because he's all political since Jeannie.

White Elk's the kid's name with the junkyard kidney, the basketball player, but the way Junior said it, all fast and smushed together, was how they'd misspelled it on White Elk's jersey at the front of the season, and how everybody's been spelling it ever since.

The girl smiled to finally hear it. "Like these," she said, nodding through the windshield at the last of the elk.

"These are *brown*," Junior said, giving the word out slow and stupid because he's Junior and thinks he's funny, but Doby in the backseat was just shaking his head slow now, and looking deep into that ratty floorboard.

"You're from—from..." Doby tried to say, and the girl waited to see if he could get to it, then just finished it for him, said "Not here, right?"

She shrugged right, yeah, sure.

Doby looked over to her.

"Sees Clear," he repeated, and she nodded back, shrugged one more time, but not so flip about it anymore. It was something about Doby's voice, Chris said, and the way the girl was looking at him it was like she was remembering him from some wayback powwow or something, when they were both on their moms' hips, and then Doby nodded to himself all at once, nudged the bundle he'd been carrying across to her a little.

"What?" she said. "Special delivery?"

"Indian mail," Doby said, trying to smile but just touching his mouth on both sides like he was nervous instead, and what I told Malory happened next is that when he looked over at her then it was like he'd been waiting a hundred years to see her, and this crazy ass Ledfeather girl all the way from

Standing Rock, she looked off after the elk and then back at Doby through her hair, like she'd maybe been waiting for him too, but was scared a little, wanted to be sure, so Doby opened his mouth and said her name across the backseat of Junior's cab, *Claire*, like a flower opening in his mouth, and she held her lips together and nodded thank you to him, yes, thank you, and then swallowed what was in her throat and just let the sides of their hands touch together again some like it didn't really matter.

But it did.

Author Note

This all started with a misheard Def Leppard lyric and a true and abiding love for June Morrissey. The lyric is from "Animal." Since 1987, I'd been hearing it as 'I remember you.' It's a mumbled nothing-line, comes right after 'We are the hungry ones on a lightning raid / Just like a river runs, like a fire needs a flame.' Then the almost-whispered *I remember you.* Even when your speakers are blown and your windows down and everybody's singing all over the song and kicking the seats and tearing out the headliner, it's perfect. Except what Joe Elliott's really saying there is 'Oh, I burn for you.' But maybe that's not so different. And June, June on her honeymoon with Gordon. June, walking into that Easter snow, forget the jacket. I still carry a doorknob for her, yeah. I don't know what it opens. But a mumbled line and a character don't make a novel. For me, Doby Saxon happened all at once. Me and my dad and cousins and uncles were hunting one week, and me and my dad slipped back into Browning, wound up trolling the college bookstore. Maybe it was a warm place to be where we didn't have to buy anything, I don't remember. But there on the shelves was this big spiralbound government report some professor had required. And it was more money than I had, sure, everything is, but I got it anyway, and wound up spilling elk blood all over it, and some of mine too. But it came off. It's *A Historical Report on the Blackfeet Reservation in Northern Montana*, by Thomas Wessel, who also provided the seed image of another one of my novels. This report though, man, it's some pretty boring, dry stuff. Unless, say, that's your people. I inhaled it. But Doby, he was still just a name that wouldn't leave my head, had been lodged there since 2001 already. When he became real for me was later that week, standing in the Game Office to get some transfer tags. Buried on the bulletin board was this old yellowy snapshot of a moose skeleton and a human skeleton mixed together. And there was no story for it. It had just shown up in some old file. But there was a story — *is* a story. Doby Saxon's, Francis Dalimpere's. Yellowtail's. Claire's. ~~Asael's~~ *Jamie's*. My brother Spot, smiling over to me twenty years ago, which is yesterday, a sheetrock knife in his hand, to open his wrist. And my granddad again, Sam, but born Francis. And yeah, I had to play a little fast and loose not just with the Wessel, but with the reservation, but I don't feel bad about that either. The truth is never in the facts. That's not to say I didn't have all kinds of help trying to get this close enough to right, though. First and always, my editor Brenda Mills, then Rob Bass and Toni Jensen for early reads, and Erica Cooper and Samuel Adam Williams for word-by-word reads, and my dad Dennis and my sister Jenny, for helping me run down information, and my great uncles and okay cousins, Pat and John and Delwyn and Lydale, all Calf Lookings, and Gayle Skunkcap, Jr., for getting me that picture, and Marvin Weatherwax for some words, and my sister Katie for Marvin, and Gerry Calf Looking, for keeping me from shooting a bear once, but letting me blast everything else. And Zinnie too, for telling me twice, like I just really needed to know, about this guy trying to get run over out by Starr School one night. It made me always wonder what he looked like, flashing into those headlights. Until now, I mean. But still, any mistakes, they're mine, and probably not even intentional. Too, the first draft of this, I had it not written by me, but LP Deal, from my last FC2 book. Just because it feels like a story he could tell. Not me, anyway. Or, not anymore. Not since the third story I ever got published, a story for Nancy, who would be my wife, a story about this pregnant girl and her boyfriend, who isn't perfect. But she burns for him, she believes in him.

    It's enough.